# Portrait of a Murder

*A Gabriella Alegré Mystery*
*Book 2*

# Portrait of a Murder

*A Gabriella Alegré Mystery*
Book 2

# Bob Seay

Thank you to Ginger Seay, Robin Seay, Lisa Culpepper, Mary Breslin, Danny DeCillis, and everyone else who read my various snippets, rewrites, and abandoned storylines.

This book is dedicated to all artists everywhere, whatever your medium of artistic expression may be. Thank you for bringing your vision to our world.

Portrait of a Murder/ Bob Seay
ISBN: 979-8-9867587-0-1

# TABLE OF CONTENTS

# One

I met Avyanna Menken on a Monday, that most auspicious of days.

After six months in Boulder, I thought I knew my new home fairly well. But, because I am not a morning person, I did not know about the incredibly brilliant Boulder sunrises. It took some time, but I eventually got out of bed early enough to learn what every native Boulderite grows up knowing: The Flatirons look best at sunrise. The giant red sandstone slabs become iridescent when the sun first hits them. Those same rock formations turn into jagged black silhouettes as the sun goes behind the mountains in the evening.

Mornings were best.

Once I learned about sunrise on the Flatirons, I started getting up at four-thirty every morning and heading out for my cart on Pearl Street where later in the day I would draw caricatures and portraits of tourists, shoppers, and children who wouldn't sit still. I had the entire four-block, pedestrian-only section of the street to myself in the early morning. The other buskers – the musicians, magicians, living statues, and other outdoor performers that made Pearl Street such an interesting place – wouldn't come out until later.

I'd set up my easel, decide whether I wanted to spend my quiet time drawing or painting, and settle in for a relaxed period of contemplative creativity. Thanks to this routine, I had four new paintings for sale at the semi-prestigious Gallery by the River in Denver. I'd already sold five paintings there. People don't need to know that my boyfriend bought three of those. Besides, Noah wasn't my boyfriend at the time anyway.

Amara, my friend, roommate, and fellow street performer, kept telling me I could avoid sleep deprivation by taking pictures of the Flatirons at sunrise and painting from those. But it's not the same. With photographs, you're no longer painting a picture of the sunrise or whatever it is you're trying to capture. You're painting a picture of a picture. You're stuck with that perspective and those colors. Another person's focus. Someone else's emphasis.

I prefer to choose my own point of view.

I was reminded of how much I disliked painting from a picture when I painted a portrait of Pello, another busker friend. I had no choice, since Pello was no longer with us. I thought – hoped – that painting his portrait would bring some sense of closure to his death and the ensuing craziness. It did not. I may have solved the case, but there was still no resolution for me. I knew the "who" and the "how" of what happened. I even had a superficial explanation for "why" that was strong enough for a conviction when the case went to trial. But I had no sense of resolution. Painting Pello was cathartic. I needed to do that painting. But it wasn't enough.

Art was a form of meditation for me. I sometimes lost sight of that on the busy days, as I cranked out three caricatures an hour, sometimes more, along with the occasional more upscale portrait. But there were no shoppers or tourists at five in the morning. No customer caricatures to draw, no non-paying kids to shoo away. The only thing open on Pearl Street at that hour was Gamma's Cupcakes, which was owned and operated by the aforementioned boyfriend, Noah Townsend. The name, which always reminded me of radiation rays, came from what Noah called his grandmother when he was very young and couldn't pronounce "grandma". Noah's coffee and breakfast muffin customers weren't interested in having their portraits drawn, at least not until they'd had their coffee. My mornings, literally and metaphorically, were a blank page.

On that Monday morning, my meditation was interrupted by an elegant looking older woman who stopped by my cart just as the sun was halfway over the horizon. In other words, just as the light on the Flatirons was perfect. She carried a muffin from Gamma's in one hand and a hiker's water bottle in the other.

"Are you the artist who did the paintings in the cupcake shop?" she asked between crumbling bites.

"I am. I'm Gabriella Alegré," I said as politely as I could without looking away from my painting.

"I'm Avyanna Menken." Her voice was thin and slightly slurred, like maybe she'd had a minor stroke or she was a little hungover. I watched her from the corner of my eye as I kept painting.

She seemed a little wobbly. Not falling over, but noticeably unsteady on her feet.

My uninvited guest took another long drink from her water bottle, presumably to give me time to fully appreciate to whom I was speaking and to respond or genuflect accordingly. But I hadn't been in Boulder long enough to recognize the name. At that moment, she was someone who was rudely interrupting my morning ritual; the human equivalent of a gust of wind or one of the dozen species of mosquitoes that call Boulder home.

"Those paintings and drawings in the bakery are quite good, almost gallery quality work," she continued. "I did not expect to find something like that in a cupcake shop on Pearl Street." Mrs. Menken finished her muffin before she spoke again. "I especially liked the three of the dancer."

"That's Amara," I said, still without looking in her direction. "She's a friend of mine." I sat up on my stool and stared at the single swipe of blue paint I'd managed to get on the paper. "She'll be around later. She's one of the living statues." Amara's *Young Bride Throwing Her Bouquet* was one of the most popular living statues on the mall. If only all my models could hold a pose for as long as Amara. If only the onlookers could be that silent.

Mrs. Menken – she seemed like one of those people you do not address by their first name – put her water bottle on top of my cart, something I don't even do, and sat uninvited on the stool I used for customers. She picked up my mirror, checked her hair, makeup, and teeth. I quietly moved her water bottle to the ground so it wouldn't get knocked off my cart. I take no chances with my paint and paper.

"Draw a portrait of me," she said.

I gave up on my painting and mentally clocked in to work at 5:47AM.

"Yes, ma'am."

Normally I would ask what pose the customer liked, whether they wanted a drawing or a painting; acrylics, pencils, or markers; all that. Maybe pastels if they wanted a soft, gauzy kind of look. But Mrs.

Menken didn't seem like someone who liked to waste time. And I wanted to get back to my sunrise, my mountains… my "me time." I pushed the easel I was using aside and pulled my other easel out from behind my cart. Rather than ask whether she wanted charcoal or Contés markers, I went with the media that was already on my palette.

Watercolors.

Watercolors do not get the respect they deserve. That's probably because they're the first experience most of us have with painting when we are children, with tiny brushes and those little white plastic trays that are impossible to keep clean. No matter how hard you tried, your painting ended up looking like a tie-dyed shirt. All the colors eventually mixed into little brown blobs because we weren't taught how to clean the brush or the palette. No wonder so many people think they can't paint. We teach them they can't paint at an early age by frustrating them with low-quality art supplies and no instruction.

"Do you do oil painting?" Mrs. Menken asked while she looked at my watercolor palette.

"I do, but oils don't work out here on the street," I explained. "They take too long to dry."

"So, what will you be using for this?"

"Watercolors."

"Oh." She rolled her eyes and raised her eyebrows. Clearly, she did not approve. *Good,* I thought. I wanted to get the Flatirons while the light is still good. I hoped she would be insulted and walk away, but I did my best to keep smiling while she considered the offer.

"OK," she finally agreed. Apparently, watercolors weren't the deal breaker I hoped they'd be. "Let's see how it looks. But I will not pay unless I like the way it turns out."

"I think you'll love this," I said, "but it's going to look great in Gamma's if you don't."

"Gamma's?" she said. "You mean that cupcake place?" She suddenly turned very serious. "You can't do that. I can't have a picture of me, no matter how well it is done, hanging up in a place like that. What would people think?"

"That you enjoy the wholesome goodness of fresh baked goods?" I suggested.

"Exactly! It would be an endorsement. Can't have that."

I allowed myself a small chuckle. "You'll see. It'll be great." I put the colors I needed on my palette. "You can do some beautiful things with watercolors."

I found the paper I was looking for and put it on the easel. The quality of paper really matters when you're using watercolors. That was one more thing that was working against us in First Grade when we smeared watery paint on waterlogged pages of coloring books. I'd been using a 100% cotton rag, 140-pound paper. That paper is not too rough but not so smooth that the colors slide around. It's a little expensive, but well worth it.

I liked red sable brushes with short wooden handles, another upgrade from the little nylon brushes we licked clean in First Grade. I had a set of seven watercolor paintbrushes with different shapes and sizes, but the size 6 round brush was becoming my favorite. The #6 is a good general-purpose watercolor brush. I used smaller brushes for details, larger for bigger areas like the sky.

I started painting. Mrs. Menken made a remarkable model, with good posture for an older woman and a strong, slightly elevated chin. She sat absolutely still and held the same pose. If it wasn't for the occasional tremor in her hands, Mrs. Menken would have made an excellent living statue.

I kept painting. I had a minor accident on her neck, but I turned it into a necklace of black pearls. The final painting looked great.

"Give it fifteen minutes to dry," I told her. "Then you can take it." I turned to my model in time to catch a glimpse of excitement on her face before it vanished. Sitting with a customer and literally watching paint dry can be awkward. I usually suggest that they go get a cup of coffee or something, but Mrs. Menken didn't seem like the kind of person who could be brushed off easily. Besides, she kept looking at me. Each glance felt more intense than the first. She raised one hand.

"Oh." She relaxed from the pose and leaned back a little. "I know who you are!" Mrs. Menken's eyes crinkled at the corners as she gave a self-congratulatory nod, with one thin, slightly shaking finger pointing at me. "You're the artist who figured out who killed that flute player, aren't you?"

"Pello. His name was Pello." I felt my chest rise and fall. "And, yes, I am that artist."

"I heard about that," she said. "Have you solved any more murder cases?"

I shook my head politely to indicate I had not, but I absolutely did not want to have another conversation about Pello, his flute, or any of the rest of it. And I certainly did not want any more "cases."

"Would you like a frame for your portrait?" I asked. "I have these paper frames here."

Mrs. Menken dug in her purse and pulled out her wallet. "There's no need for a frame. Roll it up when it's dry and put it in a tube." She handed the money for her portrait to me. "You do have tubes, right? Good. I'll have it framed at the art shop." She inspected the picture once more. "This is quite good. I didn't know watercolors could look like this."

"Thank you." I rinsed out my paint brush in a cup I kept in my cart. "I'm glad you like it."

"I was led to believe I would. Good to see my friend was right." She tried to stand but was unsteady on her feet. For a moment, she lost her balance and almost fell over. I caught her elbow and helped her sit back down.

"Thank you. I'll try that again in a few minutes." Mrs. Menken seemed a little embarrassed and somewhat confused. "Sorry. Don't know what's gotten into me lately. I get dizzy like sometimes. Thank you." She forced a smile as she regained her in-command composure. "Where was I? Oh, yes. I'm a good friend of Julia Townsend. I told her I wanted a family portrait and she recommended you. I knew she was right when I saw your work at Gamma's Cupcakes this morning."

Julia Townsend was Noah's grandmother. Noah opened Gamma's Cupcakes about four months ago. He introduced Julia to me as his grandmother and business partner. She told me to call her "Gamma."

Mrs. Menken continued. "I have five daughters and they are all in town this week. It's the first time they've been together since their father's funeral four years ago. I told them I did not want to wait until the next funeral to see all of them together again, especially since the next funeral is most likely to be mine. Since all of them are here, I thought it would be a good time to do a family portrait. In oil."

*Did she actually just offer me a job? A real commission?* I have to admit I did not see that coming. "What did you have in mind?" I asked. "How many people would be in the picture?"

"It has to be big enough for my five daughters and me. Six people altogether."

*In other words, it would be enormous.* I reached for my phone and pulled up the calculator.

"Don't bother," Mrs. Menken said. "I can tell you the dimensions. I want the painting to be seventy-two inches wide by forty-eight inches tall. That should be big enough for all six of us, right?"

"Wait," I said, holding up my hand. "Mrs. Menken. First, thank you. But a gallery-quality family portrait like what you want could take hundreds of hours. And the cost!" I punched in the numbers like they taught me at the Art Institute.

"What did you say? 72x48? That's 3,456 square inches." Now the awkward part. How much should I charge per square inch? I never

knew what that number should be. I used $4 a square inch for my paintings at The Gallery by the River and at Noah's. Should I try for $4.50 on this? Maybe $5.00? I punched the numbers into my calculator. Then I rounded it up because I like zeroes.

"How about $17,000?" I said.

"My, you are proud of your work." The more experienced businesswoman laughed. "I was thinking more like $13,000. That seems to be in the ballpark."

Thirteen thousand dollars was more money than I'd ever made on a painting. And, best of all, there would be no Gallery commission

cost. I wouldn't have to split the money with anyone! But I couldn't help going for more.

"The problem is that I can't work on anything else while I'm painting this," I explained. I tried to do that *"but I really want to make this deal"* face I'd seen in car dealerships. Unfortunately, I didn't have a manager I could pretend to go talk to.

"I could do it for $16,000."

Mrs. Menken either winked or had an involuntary eye twitch. I couldn't tell. "I like your attitude," she said. "Too many people in this world don't know what they're worth. Let's say $15,000. I will pay half upfront and the other half when it's finished." Her voice was suddenly all business. "And I will only pay that second half if I am satisfied with the painting."

"Sounds good to me." I reached out to shake her hand and noticed the thinness of her skin. "I would be honored to paint your family portrait."

"Very good," she said. She handed me a photograph. "I want it to be posed like this." It was a pretty standard family picture, the matriarch seated front and center surrounded by her daughters, each of whom looked beautiful, successful, and very, very well-monied.

Mrs. Menken may have been rich, but she was still a parent. A broad, happy smile appeared as she pointed to the middle-aged brunette standing directly behind her in the picture, her hands resting on her mother's shoulders.

"That's Alyssa, our oldest," she said. "She's an attorney. Two kids, a boy and a girl." Mrs. Menken looked at me and tapped on the picture. "Smart," she beamed. "Very smart.

And this…" the proud mother pointed to the woman standing at the right end of the lineup. "This is Theresa. She still lives here in Boulder. She has her own consulting business." She turned to me. "Very high-level clients." She took a long moment and admired her picture.

"I wish Theresa would do something about those gray streaks in her hair. She would look years younger if she colored that, don't you think?"

"Maybe." I looked at the picture more closely. "But it looks good on her. If she was a man, you'd say she was distinguished. That's a good look for a business consultant."

I could tell Mrs. Menken was not accustomed to people disagreeing with her. "Perhaps." She squinted at the picture again. "It makes her look older than she is. I'm not old enough to have a daughter that old!" she laughed.

Mrs. Menken tapped her finger on the image of the tallest sister, a strong, athletic looking woman with long, cascading curls in a chocolate raspberry color, standing at the opposite end of the line from Theresa. "This is Jerica, my middle child." The older woman turned her face to mine, then back to the picture. "She went through some hard times, but she's doing better. I'm very proud of her. It's not easy to turn your life around like she has." The remaining two women were sitting on the floor with their legs curled under them. They seemed considerably younger than their sisters. "And that's Destiny and Valena," Mrs. Menken said softly as she pointed to them. "They're twins. Alyssa was seventeen when they were born." She smiled before she explained. "It was almost two separate families." She grinned. "One husband, one father, but two separate families."

"Looks like a happy group," I said. The separation within the family was emphasized by the physical attributes of the women. The older daughters were tall. The twins, in contrast, were much shorter and more petit. And were those peach highlights in Valena's blonde hair? Nice touch.

"Valena certainly stands out with that blond hair," I said. All four of her sisters had darker hair, or at least darker hair dye.

"That blonde hair comes from my mother," Mrs. Menken said. "Ah, Valena. She's still trying to figure out what she wants to be when she grows up. That's our fault for raising her and Destiny like we did. By the time they came around, my dear husband and I were older. We were tired. I'm afraid we were much less strict with them than we were with the other three."

"She still might come around," I said. "How old are the twins?"

"Twenty-four," she said. "Destiny, the other twin, makes videos or films or something that she puts online." Mrs. Menken's chest rose and fell with a heavy sigh. "She's also still trying to figure out what she wants to be when she grows up."

I smiled and took the picture from Mrs. Menken. "Thank you. This will be very helpful," I told her. I thought I could use the picture to draw the outline of where everyone was sitting and paint the details when they posed in person. That's what da Vinci did it when he painted *The Last Supper,* except he didn't have a photograph as a reference. He had an overall idea of the form and brought the models in one at a time to fill it in. I hoped this wouldn't take me three years like it took da Vinci.

"Why don't you come by my place this evening, say around seven, and we'll have dinner?" Mrs. Menken said. Without asking, she picked up a pencil and a piece of paper from my cart and wrote her address with very shaky handwriting. "Here," she said as she held out the paper. "You can meet everyone, they can meet you, and we can set up some kind of schedule for all these portrait sittings we're going to need. And bring your friend the dancer, the one that's in those paintings. I'd like to meet her."

"Amara?" I asked.

"Is that her name? Yes, bring Amara." Mrs. Menken assessed the watercolor portrait still on my easel. "Do you think it's dry?" she asked.

It had been over fifteen minutes. More importantly, it felt dry. I carefully rolled up the paper and placed the painting in a tube. "Here you go. On the house."

"Oh no, dear." She smiled and shook her head slowly. "Never give away for free what you can sell for money. You worked on this and you earned it. Is fifty dollars enough?"

"It's usually thirty-five," I said.

"Well, now it's fifty." She put the money in my hand. "And I will see you and your friend this evening!"

I'm not sure how, but I managed to wait until Mrs. Menken walked down the street past Noah's place before I grabbed my art supplies and ran home. I also picked up the water bottle that she forgot and left behind. "No problem," I told myself, "I'll take it to her tonight."

If I planned on painting this portrait, I had to get in shape. Not physically in shape, although I could have used more physical activity in my life. I had to get in shape as a portrait artist. That may sound odd coming from someone who drew portraits and caricatures for a living, but it was true. I had not painted with oils in at least six months; not since I got my busker's license and set up my cart on Pearl Street.

People have this idea that an artist can move from one medium to another with no trouble at all, but each tool, whether it's oils, acrylics, watercolors, pencils, or whatever has its own set of challenges. Each requires its own technique. Each requires practice, which is what I had to do.

It also requires supplies. I did a quick inventory of what I had on hand. I had all the oil paints, mineral spirits, and paint thinner I needed. All the right brushes were there, including a set of Winsor & Newton hog hair brushes that were perfect for oil painting. "Nice to see you again," I said as I inspected the bristles. "It's been a while. Oink, oink."

Canvas was the only thing I didn't have. Since I started painting on Pearl Street, I had almost exclusively painted on paper. A pre-stretched 72x48 inch linen canvas – you would never paint something like this on paper – was over $500. At that price, I couldn't afford to make a mistake. I also needed paper that could handle oil paints and smaller canvases to get my oil painting chops back in shape before I started on the big picture. I put that on the shopping list for the art store.

Amara came home a few hours later, still dressed as *The Bride*. "I went by your cart," she said. "But, alas, you were not there."

"You're not going to believe what happened!" I told her. "I drew a portrait of this random woman and now she wants me to draw her entire family! My first real commission!"

"Great," Amara said. "Do you by chance remember this woman's name? That might be important."

"Avy… something." I tried to recall the name, but it was not common. "Avyanna? I think? It was a different sounding name." I tried to remember the name of my benefactor. Then it came to me. "Avyanna Menken. That's it. She was Avyanna Menken."

Amara picked up Miss Marple, our cat, from the couch and collapsed into the soft cushions beside me. Her eyes and her mouth were wide open.

"You met Avyanna Menken?" Amara whispered with awe as she ran her fingers through the cat's thick fur. My roommate and best friend shook her head before she continued. "I've lived here all my life and I've never met Avyanna Menken." She then told me about Mrs. Menken and how her late husband's family built their fortune mining for gold in the mountains before Colorado was even a state.

"She kind of married into money," Amara said. "Old, inherited, generational, family money. Everyone in Boulder knows who Avyanna Menken is."

"Just like everyone knew about the Flatirons at sunrise?" I replied. "I think you overestimate the power of this 'everybody knows' collective consciousness of yours. But that's not the best part. Not only did I meet her, but she liked my drawings of you, the ones hanging in Gamma's."

"She did?" Amara beamed like she was accepting an award. "Avyanna Menken liked me? She really, really liked me?" She feigned fainting on the couch.

"Not only that, but Avyanna Menken wants me to paint a portrait of her family. She invited you and me to come over for dinner at her house to meet everyone. Tonight."

Amara screamed. I was apparently about to introduce her to Boulder royalty and I hadn't even known it.

# Two

"Look at these houses," Amara said as out Uber carried us higher into the foothills. "Nothing in this neighborhood sells for less than five million. That's like five times the average price of a home in Boulder. And they get more expensive as you go higher."

Amara saw houses. I saw potential future clients, courtesy of Mrs. Menken. "Her friends will see the portrait and will want one of their own," I told Amara.

"Hmm… I'm not sure it works that way at this level," Amara said.

"Sure it does," I said. "Why do you think people buy Teslas?"

We arrived at Menken Manor, as Amara immediately dubbed the estate, a little after seven and were greeted at the door by a well-dressed brunette with a distinguished looking bit of gray at the temples and a half-empty drink in her hand. I recognized her from Mrs. Menken's family photograph.

"I'm Theresa. I'm glad you're here!" Her drink sloshed in her glass as she waved us in. "Come in, come in. Which one of you is the artist?"

"I am," I said. "I'm Gabriella Alegré. And this is my friend, Amara Chatterly." More than anything, the house resembled a large hunting lodge, complete with a trophy moose head on one wall and an elk head on another. Amara stopped gawking at the rustic décor long enough to say hello to our host before she wandered off for a self-guided tour.

"Nice to meet you both!" Theresa said. "I am excited about this portrait!"

"Me too," I said. "And I just realized I should have brought your mother's water bottle with me. She left it at my cart this morning."

Theresa rolled her eyes and shook her head. "She's always losing those things, but she insists on carrying them around. Don't worry about it."

Our host took my elbow and walked me around the room. "That's Alyssa," she said pointing to a very professional looking woman coming down the spiral stairway, "and that's Destiny." Theresa turned to me. "Alyssa is the tall one. And Destiny has the camera." Destiny's all black outfit and with black lace leggings and corresponding dramatic makeup was much more jarring than what she wore in the picture. She also wore a nose ring and had a silver stud in her right eyebrow, neither of which could be seen in the family photograph. All of this was topped off with a wide brimmed black fedora, complete with a peacock feather. Her mother must have asked her to tone down the darkness for the picture.

Theresa turned to me and rolled her eyes. "Destiny is always making videos, either with her phone or that camera. It's annoying and extremely distracting." I looked at Destiny. Of all the things to notice about the goth Menken daughter, the camera was the least distracting.

My host pointed and took another sip of her drink. "Valena is there on the couch," she said. The peach highlights in Valena's blonde hair were even more prominent in this light, especially when she had her head tilted down to look at her phone. No piercings.

Theresa emptied her glass and motioned to her younger sister.
"And those two are twins?" I asked. They were certainly the same size. Neither one of them could have weighed much more than ninety pounds. At barely five feet tall, these were small women.

"Identical twins," Theresa said. "Not that anyone could ever tell. They do all they can to not look alike." She took the last drink from her glass. "Valena, come here please. Be a dear and find out what Gabriella and her friend would like to drink and get it for them. Thank you."

"I'm good," I said. "But thanks." Amara was wandering around the room before Valena had a chance to ask her what she might like to drink. I was still looking at the intentionally non-identical identical twins. Mrs. Menken had mentioned how Valena got her blonde hair from her grandmother. Destiny covered her grandmother's genetic contributions in dark eggplant black. Their wardrobe choices were just as distinctive.

Theresa used the hand that was holding her drink to point to another sister. "That's Jerica, the one who just came in from the kitchen." Jerica wore a long black dress with a pearl necklace in the photograph. She looked much more at home tonight in jeans, a red and black flannel shirt, and boots. Her hair was still that beautiful chocolate raspberry color that complemented her skin tone so perfectly.

"And right behind her are her husband, Carson Culbert, and Alyssa's husband, Oswald Duncan. Oswald is the bald one." Carson's hair, in contrast to his brother-in-law's baldness, was thick and dark and perfectly styled in an Ivy League gentleman's haircut.

Oswald put a hand on Carson's arm and let Jerica get sufficiently out of earshot. The two men walked by me without saying anything, but they stopped only a few feet from where I was standing.

"Everything okay?" Oswald asked his brother-in-law. I couldn't help overhearing what he was saying. They were that close.

"Just a difference of opinion." Carson looked up at the ceiling and then at the floor. "That's all it is."

Oswald laughed and put his hand on Carson's shoulder. "Don't worry. We've all been there."

Theresa scanned the room and then turned back to me. "That's everyone except Mother. She's around here somewhere. Probably in the kitchen getting in the way. I should go get her."

I was excited about the idea of painting this family, but I was regretting the coffee I had before I came over. "I'm sorry," I said quietly to Theresa. "I know we just got here, but where is the bathroom?"

"No problem." Theresa pointed across the room. "The closest one is down the hall on the left," she said.

I overheard Carson and Jerica arguing as I made my way to the bathroom. It was hard not to. I slowed my semi-frantic pace in case Jerica needed me, although Jerica looked like the kind of woman who could hold her own in a barroom brawl without breaking a sweat.

"Did you at least talk with her about it?" Carson said.

Jerica was adamant. "I did not and I am not going to," Jerica told him. "And you are not going to either. Why do you keep asking me this?" Jerica pivoted away from her husband and walked back into the kitchen. Carson, still fuming, went in a different direction.

I found the bathroom door and stepped inside. The bathroom was actually two rooms. The first room had a large, slipper-shaped clawfoot bathtub in the center of the space. Along one wall was a long marble countertop with his and hers sinks and mirrors on three sides. There was a walk-in shower in one corner. I presumed the bathroom fixture I needed was behind another door at the far end of the room.

I knocked and then opened the second door only to find Mrs. Menken in the fetal position on the floor. She was not breathing. I immediately thought of Pello. This was a *deja vú* experience I did not want to relive.

"Theresa!" I screamed. I tried to think of another name to call out. "Alyssa! Anybody! Come here!" I checked for a pulse but found none. I started CPR anyway. I was not going to be the one to tell this family they had lost their mother.

"Someone?" I screamed as loudly as I could while I kept pumping. "Anyone?" They taught us to sing "Stayin' Alive" for a tempo for CPR. Coincidentally, that's the same tempo as "Another One Bites the Dust." I wasn't sure which song I was singing to myself when I started. I hoped I had not sung the wrong song if anyone was listening.

Then again, if they were listening, why weren't they coming to help?

After a minute that seemed more like an eternity, Alyssa and Oswald ran into the small room, followed by Theresa, then Destiny. Alyssa pushed me aside and dropped to the floor sobbing, her arms spread out over her mother. The more athletic Jerica shoved her sister out of the way and continued CPR.

"Someone call the ambulance," Jerica yelled as she kept pumping her mother's chest. "Does anyone know how long she's been down?"

"Got it," Valena said from the hallway. Valena had already dialed 911 while everyone else was running to the bathroom. She was on the phone with Mrs. Menken's personal physician by the time Jerica was screaming for someone to get an ambulance. For someone who's mother was either dead or dying, Valena was remarkably aware of what needed to be done and incredibly calm about doing it.

Jerica kept pumping hard until the paramedics arrived. Everyone stepped out of the way so the paramedics could work on Mrs. Menken. Jerica, exhausted and emotionally drained, collapsed outside the door of the second room.

The paramedics' sense of urgency disappeared quickly once they examined their patient. One of them stood up slowly as he turned to Alyssa.

"I'm sorry," said the paramedic. "There's nothing we can do here."

"What do you mean?" Alyssa asked.

"She's dead, ma'am."

# Three

The color drained from Alyssa's face. "Can we wait until the doctor is here to make that determination?" she said. "No offense, but I would feel better if a doctor made that call."

"I understand," said one of the paramedics as the other resumed chest compressions. The sisters and Oswald squeezed in closer, but most stayed in the bathtub room of the bathroom suite. I was suddenly intruding on a very private family moment. I backed up into the hallway where Amara was standing.

"What happened?" Amara whispered.

"I opened the door to the bathroom and Mrs. Menken was lying there on the floor," I told her quietly. I realized I was staring straight ahead through the open bathroom doors at the people still in the room. She's dead, Amara." I turned to my friend. "Mrs. Menken is dead and I'm the one who found her." I had a sinking feeling of *Here we go again. Pello 2.0.*

Amara and I were still in the hallway, right outside the door of the bathroom suite, but we could hear the family and occasionally see into the room, depending on where people were standing. Some of the sisters cried, others talked to their mother as if she could still hear them. The police arrived and walked quickly past us without saying anything. Close behind the police marched the man I assumed was Mrs. Menken's personal physician, Dr. Kurt Hickner. The young doctor examined Mrs. Menken. I moved in closer to hear.

"Was she like this when you got here?" the doctor asked the paramedics.

"Yes," one of them whispered. "Not breathing and non-responsive. I didn't call time of death because the family wanted you to see her first."

From the hallway, I could see the doctor checking Mrs. Menken's dilated pupils and her pulse before putting his stethoscope into his ears. Dr. Hickner looked up at the paramedic and gave a short,
barely noticeable head shake to confirm what the family already knew. Then he looked at his watch.

"Time of death, 7:34PM." The crying grew more intense.

One of the paramedics entered the time on a tablet. "Should I call the medical examiner?"

"Why?" asked Dr. Hickner as he put away his stethoscope. "You only call the ME when it's an unattended death or there is something suspicious. She was my patient. She had history of coronary artery disease. There is no evidence of foul play. There is no need to call the medical examiner."

The young paramedic disagreed. "It was an unattended death. He's going to want an autopsy."

"Autopsy?" Jerica heard the discussion from the hallway and quickly went back into the bathroom. "Is that absolutely necessary?" She turned to Dr. Hickner. "She was found dead in her bathroom. Now you want to cut her open? For what? Let her at least keep that much of her dignity."

The doctor glanced at the paramedic and mouthed the words, "Told you."

Valena shook her head and mouthed the word "No" before she spoke. She also stepped forward. "No," she repeated loudly enough for everyone to hear. Everyone was looking at her. "There should be an autopsy." She looked at Destiny for support. "Don't you think, Destiny? Shouldn't there be an autopsy?"

Destiny put down her camera and stopped recording. She looked back and forth between her mother and Valena. She turned to Theresa and then to Alyssa as if she was searching for some directions about what to do. Then she left the room and ran up the spiral stairs without saying anything. No one, other than me, seemed surprised or concerned by Destiny's reaction.

Carson put his arm around his wife's waist and pulled her close. "Avyanna would not have wanted an autopsy," he said. He looked at the faces circled around the fallen matriarch. "The family does not want an autopsy." With the exception of Valena, there was no disagreement.

Dr. Hickner looked around the circle of faces and the stunned eyes looking back at him. "There will be no autopsy," he said flatly. "This death is from natural causes. Mrs. Menken had heart problems that unfortunately led to her death. That is well documented in her medical records. She was in my office earlier this week and is on several medications for high blood pressure and other problems." The doctor turned to the paramedic.

"She was my patient. I will sign her death certificate."

Dr. Hickner put his hand on Alyssa's shoulder. "I am very sorry for your loss," he said, then he looked at each of the family members as he spoke. "For all of our loss. Your mother was quite a lady."

I watched as Valena accompanied him to the front door. They shared a long and very tight embrace.

Amara gasped then put her hand over her mouth and leaned towards me.

"Did you see that?" she whispered.

"You mean when they kissed before he left?" I said. "Yeah."

Amara kept looking at the couple in the doorway. "Would you kiss someone like that if your mother had just died?" She elbowed me. "And look where his hand is!"

"Seeking comfort in her grief, I guess."

"Uh huh," Amara said. "She's seeking something."

Valena noticed Amara and me standing in the hallway as she came back down the hall. She wiped her eyes and cleared her throat to speak.

"I'm not sure what to tell you. Obviously, our plans have changed."

I took her hands in mine. "I am so sorry." Amara and I said goodbye to Valena and walked outside to wait for our ride.

The policeman followed me out and introduced himself. "Ms. Alegré? I'm Officer Singer, Boulder Police Department."

"I thought you looked familiar," I said. Of course, I recognized him. I was hoping he'd go away. The last thing I wanted right then was the attention of some cop, amorous or otherwise, and especially not the one that arrested John Spool because he was too lazy to look for evidence.

"Listen," the officer said in a hushed voice. "No offense, Gabriella, but you seem to have a knack for finding dead people. I know the doctor said she died of natural causes, but I'd like to ask you a few questions. We can do that right here. No need to go anywhere. Where was Mrs. Menken when you walked into the bathroom?"

"She was where you saw her, lying there near the door," I said. "I did CPR. I stopped when one of her daughters – I think it was Alyssa, I just met them tonight, but it was one of the daughters – ran into the bathroom.

"And did you see Mrs. Menken go into the bathroom?"

"No." I shook my head. "I did not." I looked at Amara then back to the officer. "We'd just got here."

Officer Singer wasn't finished. "And did you hear any sounds coming from the bathroom before you went in?"

*Does he think I stand around listening for bathroom sounds?* "No," I said as slowly as possible. "I knocked on the door and there was no response. I thought the bathroom was empty. Had I thought someone was in the bathroom, I would not have opened the door. I did not expect to find Mrs. Menken, on the floor or otherwise."

The officer put down his tablet and looked at me. "I would remind you that this is a closed case. A natural death means there will be no investigation. Please do not go off on your own and break into Mrs. Menken's house the way you broke into Eos' place."

"I don't know anything about that," I said.

"Doesn't matter. We know about that. And how you broke into John Spool's place after Pello died. We know about that, too. We let it slide because, well, you were right and you found the killer."

"What you mean is I did your job for you," I reminded him.

The officer bit his lip before he spoke. "It's hard to argue with that. But we can't let it slide again, especially not with this case." He pointed to the mansion behind him. "Besides, if you broke in here, you'd be dealing with the Menken's personal security long before the Boulder PD ever showed up. They're not as nice as us."

"You're right," I said with an intentionally exaggerated eye roll. "Her doctor already said she died of natural causes." I threw up my hands and shrugged my shoulders. "I'm surprised you're asking any questions at all." I knew that people died from natural causes all the time. Maybe it was my lack of experience with death in general, but this did not feel natural.

"Standard procedure," Officer Singer said. "Glad you understand."

I just wanted the conversation to end. Fortunately, our Uber pulled up at before Officer Singer could ask anymore questions or find some other excuse to talk to me. Amara slid across the seat and Singer closed the door behind me.

"We'll be in touch," he said.

Neither Amara nor I said anything on the ride home. I think we were both just absorbing everything that happened. I know I was. It was only a ten-minute ride, so we didn't have time to say much, even if we had been in more talkative moods. Mrs. Menken's death was different from Pello's. There was no evidence of violence, no blood. No friend holding her. No last goodbyes.

Amara must have been thinking the same thing. "I guess that's what a natural death looks like," she said. We got out of the car. "It's definitely sad," she continued. "But it seems kind of anticlimactic, that's all. I guess I never thought about it. You live your life and then it's over. You just leave."

I unlocked the door to our place and picked our mail up off the floor. "I feel horrible, honestly. A woman is dead. A family has lost their mother. And I'm feeling guilty because I can't help thinking how I lost $15,000 and I still haven't made it to the bathroom." I looked into Amara's eyes. "Does that make me a bad person?"

"I don't think it makes you 'bad', necessarily," Amara said as she kicked off her shoes. "Cold and narcissistic, perhaps, but not necessarily a bad person. You're not a sociopath or anything."

"Nice to know," I said as I closed the bathroom door behind me. I could hear Amara on the other side of the door. "We got a letter from our landlord. Do you want to read it or should I?"

She handed me the envelope when I came back into the room.

"You can read it," she said.

Amara plopped down on the couch and stroked Miss Marple's thick fur. "He better not be complaining about Miss Marple, huh Miss Marple?" She held up the cat and shook him playfully. "He's not complaining about you, is he?"

"You shouldn't talk baby talk to the cat," I said. "She's going to answer you some day and we want her to speak like an adult." I tore open the envelope and started reading.

"OK, now I am grieving," I said.

"What?" Amara took the letter from my hand.

"I'll save you the trouble," I said as she read. "They're selling our house to some developer. We're going to have to move."

Amara stared at what was essentially our eviction notice. "I don't know if we can find a place as cheap as this one," she said. "Rents have gone up all around Boulder. Denver, too. I was paying less because I've lived here since college. And I think he kind of likes me."

"Higher rent. Great." I collapsed on the couch. "I'll need to draw more portraits. More caricatures. I don't know if there's that many more people to draw on Pearl Street."

Amara put her feet up on the table we kept in front of the couch. "Yeah, it's not like we can run a sale or something to attract more customers. This is not good."

I never asked Amara about her money. She always had enough for her half of the rent and the other bills, so I didn't worry about it. Besides, I was the one who moved in with her. The lease was in her name.

But I did wonder how much a living statue could make in tips in a single day, even if that statue was as popular as Amara's *Bride Throwing Her Bouquet* or her *Cowgirl With Lasso,* another crowd favorite. She'd talked about asking Noah for a job at Gamma's but that was still in the talking stage. She had not yet asked Noah for anything as far as I knew, other than a refill on her coffee. At age twenty-seven, Amara wasn't ready to give up on being a street performer.

"I don't know if I can get that many more customers each month," I said. This was August. What was it going to be like in October? January? Even if people still came outside to shop or eat, it's hard to draw much of anything when your hand is shivering from the cold. And the snow. Boulder gets more snow than any other city in the United States except for places in Alaska. What is that even like?

I wouldn't have to worry about the weather or the foot traffic on Pearl Street if I could count on sales at The Gallery by the River, but I couldn't count on that. It was great when something sold, but it's totally unpredictable and absolutely out of my control.

"I don't know if I can afford to stay in Boulder," I told Amara. I loved our little house and having Amara as a roommate. I loved the location, only one block from Pearl Street. I did not want to move. It wasn't even 8:30 yet and all I wanted to do was to go to bed while I still had a bedroom.

Amara tucked Miss Marple under one arm and reached for the jar of black jellybeans with the other hand.

"I feel bad for that family." Amara offered the jellybean jar to me.

"I know," I said. I put two or three black jellybeans in my mouth without thinking. "Mrs. Menken said that was the first time they had all been together since her husband's funeral."

Amara took the jar back and slowly sunk her hand through the jellybeans and left it there. I think she liked the way they felt on her hand, like sticking your hand into a jar of beads. "Do you think the excitement of having everyone in the house was too much for her?"

"Maybe. But…." I thought about how Mrs. Menken looked when I met her. "She would have fallen if I hadn't helped her off that stool this morning. And her speech was not right. Not drunk slurred, but something was going on there." I tried to remember more details about our encounter. "Her skin color seemed a little off. I didn't notice it when she first sat down."

I turned to Amara. "To be honest, I was trying not to look at her and hoping she would go away and I could paint the Flatirons. I noticed her skin color more when I was painting her portrait. It seemed off, a little more yellowish than most people."

Amara slowly pulled out a handful of jellybeans and put them in her mouth one at a time. "Skin color could be anything," she said. "Maybe she was a heavy drinker. Maybe she got a fake tan. That could be anything."

I sat up straighter. "It could. But all that together, the balance, the speech, the skin color… Something was going on there. Maybe that's what her doctor was talking about. He would have known if she had those problems, right?"

"One would hope," Amara said.

It was still way too early to go to bed. Why did it feel so late?

# Four

I woke up to the sound of Amara's yoga video. She's usually quiet when she knows I'm sleeping. But, to be fair, she probably didn't know I was there. Since I'd started my pre-dawn art therapy, I was usually already gone when she woke up. But it was very early. My alarm had not yet sounded. Amara must not have slept very well either.

"We should go to Noah's," I said as I wiped my eyes and made my way to the table. "Get a muffin. Something."

"Sorry. I didn't know you were here." Amara turned the video off. "I'm not sure about Noah's. I've gained seven pounds since he opened that place."

"Just coffee," I said.

"OK. Just coffee." She grabbed her shoes. "And maybe a muffin."

Gamma's Cupcakes was busy but not packed. The morning crowd tended to be commuters who were on their way to work and were picking up a muffin and coffee to go or retirees who hung out to talk to their friends. The busker crowd didn't come in for their morning caffeine fix until around ten, just as most of the other businesses were opening up. Noah's little shop had become the unofficial breakroom for the Pearl Street Buskers. It was the only place on the street where you could see the living statues out of character but already in costume before they started working. There were days when Gamma's felt more like a cosplay convention than a coffeeshop. John Spool and the other musicians usually didn't show up until later in the afternoon. Most of the musicians performed until the bars closed at night, long after the living statues and I had gone home.

Amara and I were equally familiar with both crowds.

"I saw you painting Mrs. Menken yesterday!" Noah said as he wiped his hands and followed us to a table. "Trying to get some more upscale clients so you don't have to draw the common riffraff of the street?"

"Funny." I stirred my coffee. "She seemed like a nice person. She wanted a family portrait, but it's not going to happen."

Noah sat down beside me and slowly traced a finger across the back of my hand and up my arm. "So why isn't it going to happen?"

I looked at Amara and wondered if we should tell him. It's not like it was a big secret. And it deserved to hear it in person from someone he knew instead of reading about it the paper or online somewhere. He might as well hear it from me.

I put my hand on top of Noah's. "Mrs. Menken died last night," I said.

Noah's mouth dropped open. "No kidding. Are you sure?"

"Very sure," I said. "We were there when it happened." Noah looked to Amara to confirm my story.

"Yes, we were," Amara said. "We were right there." She nodded towards me. "Nancy Drew here was the one who found the body."

"I used to go to that house when I was a kid," Noah said. "Gamma and Mrs. Menken were friends. I played with Valena and Destiny while Gamma and Mrs. Menken and some other old ladies played bridge." Noah closed his eyes. His smile, usually brilliant, became a tight downturned line. "Gamma will want to know," he said. "And I should be the one to tell her before everyone is talking about it."

"I'm sorry to be the one to tell you," I said.

"And you had no idea who she was when you painted her yesterday?" Noah asked.

"No idea at all," I said. "I could tell she was the high society type, but most of Boulder fits that description." Boulder was and remains an eclectic mix of artists, academics, hippies, and professionals. It also ranks among the wealthiest cities in North America. It's an interesting juxtaposition of people who can and cannot really afford to live there.

"Avyanna Menken was more than high society," Noah said. Amara nodded in agreement as Noah continued. "She owned a lot of land in downtown Denver."

I was confused so I turned to Amara. "I thought you said her family struck it rich in a gold mine?"

Noah was quick to confirm Amara's story. "They did. Or he did. It was like Mr. Menken's great-grandfather or someone way back there. Maybe further back than that. But the gold mining eventually dried up. The family used their gold money to buy land in what is now downtown Denver. There wasn't much to Denver back then. Their
money grew along with the city."

Now I was confused. "I thought banks and tech companies owned most of the real estate downtown."

"They do now," Noah said. "But the Menkens owned most of that before the banks moved in. And they still own the parking lots. Like I said, there wasn't much down there when his great-grandfather started buying up land. He sold off some of it to developers. The Menkens themselves never built anything except asphalt surfaces and booths for parking lot attendants."

"Mr. Menken's great-grandfather sounds like some kind of visionary, buying up all that land before Denver was even really a city," I said. "I can't imagine what all of that must be worth now. I'm surprised they didn't sell all of it."

Noah sipped my coffee without asking. I swatted his hand when he put down the cup. He explained more about the Menkens. "Mr. Menken's dad sold some of it, back when downtown started to grow. He made bank with that. And I'm sure they've had offers for the rest, especially since Mr. Menken died. That was about five years ago. Real estate has gotten even more valuable since then. But Mrs. Menken refuses to sell." He stared into my coffee cup. "Refused to sell, I guess," he said.

"Mrs. Menken said the family had not all been together at the same time since his funeral four years ago," I said. "That seems sad."

"Yeah," Noah said. "It's not an especially close-knit family."

Amara picked a chocolate chip out of her muffin. "Who knew you could make a fortune from parking lots?"

"It's not the parking," Noah said. "I mean, people pay a lot for parking. There is that. But Mr. Menken used the parking lots as collateral to get loans for other investments. Gamma told me about all this. Most of their income now, from what I understand, comes from those investments."

I recognized the pattern. "Investments they could afford to make because they leveraged the land beneath the parking lots," I said. I was beginning to understand the extent of the Menken family fortune. I wondered how it would be divided among the daughters now that Mrs. Menken was dead.

Noah looked at his phone. "It says that parking lots cover almost twenty-five percent of downtown Denver. Over nine thousand acres."

"How big is that?" I asked.

"Big," Noah said. "Very big. Parking spaces in downtown Denver – not entire lots, just *individual spaces* – are selling for between twenty-five thousand and thirty-five thousand dollars each in some parts of town. That's for one space. Imagine what an entire parking lot would be worth."

Noah was suddenly more than a little embarrassed. "Please don't ask me how I know that," he said.

Amara looked at Noah. "Did you go to Elitch's when you were a kid?" she asked Noah. Elitch Gardens was a big theme park that sat in the middle of downtown Denver. You can see the Ferris wheel from the interstate as you drive by.

"Then let's try that." I picked up my phone. "How big is Elitch Gardens in Denver?"

"Elitch Gardens is twenty-eight acres," said the voice.

I watched as Noah did the math in his head. "There it is," he said. "The Menkens own over three hundred times more land than a medium-sized amusement park."

"All in parking lots and spread out all over town," Amara said. "That's a lot of real estate."

"Speaking of real estate." I reached across the table to Amara.
"We have to go house hunting." I immediately regretted my words. I did not want Noah to know about our housing situation. But there it was, on the table along with the crumbs from our breakfast.
I was hoping that maybe Noah hadn't heard it.

He had.

"You're moving?" Noah asked.

"Yeah," Amara said. "The joy of renting. They're selling our place to some developer. We're going to have to find new accommodations."

Amara leaned on me. "Oh!" She covered her open mouth with three fingers and feigned and overly dramatic embarrassment. "Was I not supposed to say that? I am so sorry."

Noah blinked a couple of times and shook his head before he turned to me. "Is that right? They're selling your place? What are you going to do?"

"We're working on it," I said as I fake glared at Amara. "We'll figure it out." I checked the time on my phone. "If I'm going to pay more rent, than I need to draw more people." I stood up and kissed Noah on the forehead. "Sorry I had to be the one to tell you about Mrs. Menken. I hope Gamma takes the news OK." I was trying to think of anything that would keep Noah from revisiting my housing problem.

"Thanks," he said. "I'll tell Gamma this morning before she has a chance to watch the news. I'll let you know how it goes."

Amara walked with me to my cart. I held back from saying anything until we were about half way there. Noah and I had been dating for only a few months. It was a good relationship, the first truly healthy relationship I had been in in a while. Not that I'd had many relationships at all at that point. I was alone by choice, but it meant that I had spent most of my adult life thus far as a single, unattached woman.

I eventually could hold it in no more. I tapped on Amara shoulder with my fist. It was more than a fist bump, but not a full wallop.

"I can't believe you told him we had to move!" I said.

She returned the blow with equal force. "You were the one who said we were going house hunting."

"Saying we're going house hunting is not the same as telling him we're on the verge of being homeless," I argued.

"Yeah. He kind of ran with that, didn't he?" Amara laughed and rubbed her shoulder. For a moment I wondered if I had actually hurt her. "But you had to know he would find out sometime. Does it really matter when?"

I stopped walking and turned to Amara. "It matters because now he's going to ask me to move in with him. He's been hinting around about it for a month now. This is going to make that worse."

"I take it you don't want to move in?"

"No," I said. "I don't. And I can't even give him a reason for it. I just don't want to do it. Isn't that reason enough?"

"Should be," Amara agreed.

We started walking again.

"Has he heard you fart?" Amara asked out of nowhere.

"What the…?!" I didn't know what to say. I was trying not to laugh. "What kind of question is that?"

"It's a serious question," Amara insisted. "Has this man heard you fart?"

"No. Of course not. Why would I do that?"

"You can't move in with him unless you can fart in front of him. That's my rule. If I can't fart in front of the guy, I don't move in. The colon knows."

I looked at her as we kept walking. "I guess I never realized how much of your moral code was based on audible emissions of methane."

Amara was persistent. "Have you heard him?"

"Heard him what?" I stammered. "Heard him… do that? In front of me? No. He's not the kind of guy who casually rips one while he's watching professional wrestling."

"Then he's not ready either, if that's any consolation. He may think he's ready, but he's not. Not until he's comfortable enough to do that."

For the first time in this ridiculous conversation, I allowed myself to smile and laugh a little. "Kind of a sniff test, huh?"

"Exactly," Amara said. "Think of it as a way to clear the air." Amara still had to go back to the house and get dressed for her day, but I was ready to draw. Even if I had no customers. I stayed with the cart, did pencil sketches of random things on the street, and kept telling myself that I did not need to figure out whether or not Mrs. Menken was murdered.

# Five

I sat at my easel on Pearl Street and thought about the reality of my situation. Our rent was lower than any of the rentals we had seen listed. This was a classic case of "don't know what you've got till it's gone." From what I'd seen, we couldn't afford anything within walking distance of Pearl Street. We'd be lucky to find something within driving distance. And then one of us would have to buy a car. And gas.

This was not good. I tried reminding myself that I was still alive and so was my mother. Those are good things, but they did not change my situation.

We could save money by eating at home. Between Papa's Tapas and Gamma's Cupcakes, Amara and I had outsourced most of our cooking to the professionals. Although, Noah didn't charge us for half of what we ate there. That's a convenient bonus we would lose when we moved. Then again, we might also lose ten pounds each if we stopped eating muffins for breakfast and cupcakes for an afternoon snack.

I could change some things in my art cart, use cheaper paints, not provide frames. Would that hurt my sales? Would people even notice?

My recent exploration of watercolors was fun but, unlike the little trays they gave us in kindergarten, it was not cheap. The Holbein Artists' twelve-color watercolor set that I bought when I started working with watercolors again was a bargain at one-hundred twenty-five dollars. And of course I had to expand the basic palette with additional colors. At up to twenty dollars or more a piece, those weren't cheap either. Neither were the brushes. Then I discovered watercolors in tubes, which had a similarly negative economic impact. I could stop using those and just use the pans.

All of those savings could be used to cover the rent on a new place. I just have to buy cheap art supplies and never try anything new.

*"Who am I kidding,"* I thought. *"I could cut out every expense I have and still not have enough income to afford anywhere in Boulder County or Denver."*

I was pondering the economic impact of watercolor paints on my personal budget when Theresa Menken almost ran into my cart. I was deep in thought and was surprised when I heard a voice say "Hello."

I jumped a little at the sound.

"Didn't mean to interrupt," Theresa gasped. Her running outfit alone probably cost more than half my wardrobe. "I had to get out of that house. Too many people. Too much noise. And we all fall right back into the roles we had when we were growing up. Alyssa keeps ordering everyone around. That triggers Jerica's authority issues and makes Destiny and Valena withdraw even more. And Destiny's camera is recording all of this." She took a breath. "All of which makes me crazy." She tossed her head back and forth and ran her hands through her slightly graying hair.

"I'm sorry," Theresa said. "I didn't mean to vent on you like that. I wanted to talk to you about a couple of things. First, the funeral will be next Tuesday. I'll text you the details later. I know you just met Mother and didn't really know her, but you're welcome to come."

"Thank you," I said, again not knowing what to say in that kind of situation or if I would even go. Thankfully Theresa had provided a convenient escape.

"And what was the other thing?" I asked.

"Oh! I wanted to ask if you would do a portrait of me like the one you did of Mother." Theresa wiped her eyes and sniffed back some sadness. "Such a beautiful picture. Thank you so much."

"You're very welcome," I managed to say. I wasn't sure why I felt tears on my cheek.

"I was wondering if you would do a portrait of me," Theresa said. "Could you? I mean, not right now." I'm a mess. But soon, when it works for both of us. I would like that."

"I think this is a perfect look for a portrait," I said. "This is *you*, a strong, healthy, active woman. It's powerful. It's a great look."

"You think so?" Theresa looked in my mirror, touched up what little makeup she was wearing, and took a seat on my stool.

We were ready to paint. I wondered if she was ready to talk.

"I'd like a watercolor portrait, like the one you did for her," Theresa said. "Why did you choose watercolor? Isn't that kind of an unusual choice for a portrait?"

I grinned. "Well, honestly, I used watercolor because..."

"Let me guess," Theresa interrupted. "You chose watercolors because you thought Mother was a pretentious and condescending old woman and the watercolors were an ironic way to laugh at that." She turned to me. "It was a joke, right?"

I wasn't sure how I felt about one of my paintings being called "a joke." I mean, yes, I was being sarcastic when I said I would use watercolors, but I wasn't sure that I wanted Theresa or any of the rest of the family to think that I thought of their mother as a punchline. And the portrait was no joke.

"Actually," I said. "I chose watercolors because I was already set up to paint with watercolors. I was getting ready to paint the Flatirons when she came by that morning. That's why I was here early. I wanted to keep painting the Flatirons, but she was rather insistent."

"She could be that way," Theresa sighed.

"Besides," I said, "any stabbing of the pretentious and condescending, ironic or otherwise, would be a bad idea on my part. That's my target market, pretentious, condescending, and wealthy." I stirred my paints and thought about what Amara said when I got my first check from The Gallery by the River: "Congratulations! You've become another artist I can't afford."

Theresa checked her face again. "Well," she said, "I'll say it if you won't, even if she was my mother. She was unbearable at times. And judgmental?" She rolled her eyes. "You would not believe. You must have made quite an impression for her to ask you to draw that portrait. I don't know what you did, but you're good."

"I think I benefited from a recommendation from a mutual friend, Julia Townsend."

Theresa's jaw dropped but her face morphed into a big smile.

"You're friends with Julia Townsend?" she asked. "I had no idea. And you're out here painting on the street? Sounds like Jerica, rejecting the privileges of family fortune and going your own way. Making it on your own. A real starving artist. How romantic."

"Not quite," I assured her. "The art in our home came from furniture stores when I was growing up." I started picking out colors for Theresa's painting and putting them in my palette, shades of orange, gold, dark brown, and a nice warm gray for her hoodie. I mixed white, brown, and yellow to create a light almond shell skin tone, like her mother's.

Romanticism aside, Theresa was skeptical. "How do you know Julia Townsend?" she asked.

"Gamma is my boyfriend's grandmother. Noah Townsend." I flinched when I realized I had called her Gamma. I hoped Theresa hadn't noticed.

She did.

"You must be close if you call her 'Gamma'," Theresa said. "I thought Noah was the only one who was allowed to call her that. Julia is a nice lady. Incredibly rich. She and my mother were good friends." Theresa laughed. "She used to drag Noah along when she came to the house. Poor kid. Noah was five or six. I think the twins are about the same age as Noah. They'd dress up and put on little plays." Theresa laughed.

I laughed harder than I should have. "Do you have any video or pictures?"

"I wish," she said. "No. Noah's probably glad we don't."

"I bet he is."

Theresa did her best to look straight ahead, trying to be a good model but obviously needing to talk. "Alyssa hated it when Mother acted like she was Queen. And she would give it right back to her. It got nasty sometimes." Theresa stopped talking. "Jerica *really* hated it, but she went in a different direction to show that," she said much more softly.

"Jerica's the middle child, right?" I asked.

"Right. She's in the middle." Theresa adjusted her position on the stool. "When Mother got that way with us, all self-important, or

when she was being that way towards someone else, Jerica would leave. At first, when she was in high school, she would leave the room. Just walk out in the middle of a conversation and go to her bedroom or outside or somewhere. You can imagine how Avyanna Menken reacted to being ignored like that." Theresa shook her head. "Then she started leaving the house, sometimes for days. She moved out on her own before she even graduated from high school. Got a little place over in Longmont, but that wasn't enough, I guess."

Theresa took a deep, frustrated breath. "Still, Jerica managed to graduate from high school. And then she left the state." Theresa bit her lower lip and then twisted her mouth into a smile. "Moved to Montana and bought a ranch. She raises these long-haired Highland Cattle." She shook her head and chuckled softly. "My sister, raising cows. Mother did not approve."

"Your sister raises yaks?" I asked.

Theresa laughed. "Not yaks. Long-haired Highland Cattle. Their hair is like a sheep dog. That kind of hair. All black. And they really are beautiful animals, out there in their green pasture in the mountains. Quite the pastoral scene. It's a shame they all end up as hamburgers."

I felt a wave of guilt, but I was getting used to it. Carnivore shaming is a sport in Boulder.

"Wasn't Jerica's husband at the house the other night?" I remembered seeing two men. One was Alyssa's husband. The other looked like he was with Jerica.

"Yeah. She got married at some point. Some cowboy up there named Carson." Theresa chuckled a little and straightened a wrinkle in her pants. "Mother was not happy that Jerica married a cowboy. I remember her saying, 'It's bad enough she got cows. Did she have to get a cowboy, too?'." Theresa's eyes got wider and her words sped up.

"I mean a real cowboy. Jerica says he rides a horse, uses a lasso, the whole bit, although you wouldn't have known that the other night. And I've never seen him do any of that cowboy stuff. It's not like he walks around wearing a cowboy hat and spurs. Not here in Boulder, anyway." She laughed. "Mother wouldn't even attend the wedding. I did. Carson's a nice guy, I guess. Very smart. Has an MBA. Surprisingly well read. But he's not the kind of man we were supposed to marry."

Theresa made sure she had me by the eyes before she finished her thought.

"We were supposed to marry boys like Noah," she said.

I smiled at Noah's name. "I don't know. Jerica's cowboy sounds pretty manly. Your mother would have preferred a man who makes cupcakes?"

"Well, no," she conceded. "She would prefer a man who came from money. I'm not sure if how he got it matters."

"Did Jerica's cowboy come from money?"

"Are you kidding?" Theresa laughed. "I don't know where he came from, but he didn't come from money." She looked at her hands and raised her head. "Jerica and Carson are doing okay. Their house is beautiful, but it's no mansion. Most ranchers aren't rich. They may have millions in land, but they never have any cash. No liquidity, as they say. The only rich rancher is a retired rancher who managed to sell everything when he quit."

I wondered how someone like the Menken family defined "rich." Judging by their home, someone could be a millionaire and still

not qualify until their millions were in the double or maybe triple digits. Forget millions. The Menken concept of rich probably started with a "B."

"Still," Theresa dragged both of her hands downwards across her face, momentarily but completely blocking my view. "I can't believe she's gone. We were hiking Trail Ridge last week. She was happy. It was a good day."

I put some more paint on my brush. "Trail Ridge is a nice hike. I hope you brought along something for her to drink."

"I did. She'd lost her water bottle so I gave her one of mine. Again." Theresa smiled and shook her head. "She was always losing those. Always leaving them behind somewhere."

Theresa's voice got softer as she reflected on their hike and I got more involved in painting. I can talk while I paint things like the sky or some kind of single-color background. Details like someone's face require more focus. I was a little nervous, which is unusual. I couldn't tell if it was because I thought Theresa had high expectations for this portrait or if it was because I was only beginning to realize the social circles Noah must have moved in as he was growing up. The circles he probably still moved in. I suddenly suspected that his upbringing was very different from my own. Was he the Jerica of his family, running off to prove he could make it on his own, with the safety net of Gamma's money? Was I the bohemian girlfriend he needed to make the picture complete and really upset his family?

I finished Theresa's portrait. I went with bolder brush strokes than I had for Mrs. Menken. It was a dramatic look, a picture of a woman who obviously had a lot on her mind but nonetheless had hope in her eyes.

Theresa loved it.

I thought about what Theresa said after she left and I was cleaning everything up. It sounded like at least three of the sisters were not big fans of mom, or Mother, as they seemed to call her. This seemed especially odd for Theresa, the daughter who stayed close to home and, I assumed, became a kind of caregiver for her aging mother. I wasn't sure about the twins, but it sounded like they kept their distance from their older sisters. But all families have some tension, right?

Still, Theresa was criticizing her mother and the woman hadn't even been buried yet. I would have thought this would be a time to focus on happier memories. To show some love and respect for the deceased.

Maybe that's why Theresa came to visit me in the first place. All they were talking about at the house were the happy memories. For someone like Theresa, who seemed to be a very real person, that kind of historical revisionism had to be hard to hear, especially if she felt guilty about remembering the less-than-happy times and how her mother made her feel. If she was the one who stayed behind to look after their mother, which seemed to be the case, that would create even more stress and mixed emotions.

Painting is easy. People are complicated.

# Six

Saturday afternoons were prime time for the buskers. John Spool was already at his spot playing guitar and singing the blues, his Black face glistening with sweat from the sun. A new magician and another guitar player who was not nearly as good as John were also on the street, along with Amara and three other living statues. A young woman was playing different sized paint buckets as if they were drums. The four-block pedestrians-only section of Pearl Street was full of tourists and families, my target market. I could tell this was going to be a good day.

I avoided thinking about Mrs. Menken and my habit of stumbling over dead people by staying busy most of the afternoon. When I wasn't drawing caricatures and painting the occasional portrait, I watched Amara performing across the street. It was *Cowgirl* day for Amara. Not as popular as *The Bride Tossing Her Bouquet,* but still a crowd favorite. Amara's outfit and makeup were done in shades of red, orange, copper, and rust. Amara did not think of herself as an artist, but her sense of color was as good as any artist I'd ever met. Paul, another living statue and Amara's boyfriend, was going through his *Firefighter* statue poses a little further down the street. Paul had no sense of color. His statues were all marble white. Amara always said Paul should do Michelangelo's *David* as a living statue.

"He has the butt for it," Amara said. "That's all I'm saying."

I could barely hear John's music from my cart, but I could see the crowd in the street. And I could hear the applause between songs. I decided to take a break and walk over. I didn't need to talk to him, although I wasn't avoiding a conversation. I wanted to hear his music. I was there for a couple of songs before John saw me in the crowd. He smiled and waved between songs. Then he finished his set and came over to where I was sitting.

"How's it going?" John asked. The difference between John and other people was that when John asked "How's it going?", he actually wanted to hear how it was going.

"It's good," I said. "Doing some painting. Doing some drawings."

"But?" he said.

"No buts," I lied. "Life is good."

He cradled his guitar across his chest and leaned in as if to whisper a secret. "Did you hear about Mrs. Menken? I heard they found her dead in the bathroom. Like Elvis."

"Yeah," I said. He probably heard about it from one of Amara's living statue friends. Those people share everything.

"What do you think happened?" he asked.

"The doctor said it was heart failure," I told him. "Natural causes. Not much mystery there."

"But you don't think it was, do you?" John cackled and slapped his leg. "And you can't stand it." He laughed as he moved his head back and forth. "I should start taking bets on how long it will be before you break into their house and start looking around."

I was hoping that was all John had to say about Mrs. Menken. I wasn't wrong, but I wasn't ready for what he said next.

"I wanted to tell you...," John paused before finishing his thought. "I'm thinking about leaving Boulder and going back to Memphis. At least I have family there. I've been out here a long time, and I've loved it, but there's not much here for me now."

The kind but tired older gentleman sitting beside me was an exception among street performers. Most buskers quit once they realized performing on the street often meant performing for free. Very few develop the kind of following John Spool had. Even fewer made a career of it. There was a bagpipe player – complete with kilt – but he left when the restaurant owners offered to pay him for not playing near their restaurants. Several guitarists and some singers had tried their luck since Pello died, but none of them were as good or as personable as John. They were opening acts at best, warm-up bands. John Spool was still the unofficial house band of Pearl Street.

"I hate the idea of you leaving." I tried to smile. "But I understand why." Boulder was good for John because he loved Pello. With Pello gone, there wasn't much here for him to love. He just
wanted to go home.

John shifted his guitar to playing position. "Besides, the housing market is pretty hot right now. Might be a good time to sell our place before that changes. All bubbles eventually burst."

John lived right on Pearl Street, not far from my cart, in an apartment above Hempy's, a store that sold clothes made of hemp. Pello had lived there with him.

Many of the businesses on Pearl Street were originally two-story houses before the redevelopment that changed the area from residential to commercial and later to a pedestrian mall. The street-level floors of those original homes became businesses – Gamma's Cupcakes, Hempy's Clothing Store, Papa's Tapas and others – and the top floor was an apartment that either housed the businessowners or was rented out to people who made a lot more money than me.

The rumor was that Pello paid cash for the building when he and John moved out here. Based on what I knew of Pello's money, I believed it. I couldn't imagine how much the value of a property like that must have gone up in fifteen years. I also couldn't imagine ever being able to afford an upstairs apartment on Pearl Street.

It was still early on a Saturday afternoon. John looked at his watch, then at the sky that was threatening rain, and finally at the shoppers and tourists on the street. "I think I'm going to call it a day," he said. "Think I'm just going to go home."

John Spool would never have gone home like that six months ago, not in the middle of the afternoon. He would have played until the bars closed at two that night. But things were different for him now. He was more hit or miss. Other buskers were beginning to use his spot on the street when he wasn't there, another thing that would have been unheard of before.

John put his guitar away in its case and got up to leave. "I'll come by your cart sometime and we can talk," he said. "I just don't feel like being out here right now."

I went back to my cart and started sharpening my colored pencils. I talked to a few people who happened to stop by, drew a caricature of a young couple who wanted something unique to take home. A little boy wanted to be drawn in a four-panel cartoon. Those are always fun. I was finishing up a Princess Portrait of a six-year-old girl and was thinking about going home when I saw Alyssa Menken coming up the sidewalk.

"We talked it over and we decided to go ahead with the family portrait," she said. "It was Theresa's idea. She thinks that's what Mother would have wanted. I personally think it's a little creepy, but that's what we decided."

"Let me make sure I understand. You want a family portrait of the five of you?" I asked. "I would be glad to do that."

"Six, actually," Alyssa said.

"We want you to include Mother. Make it like the photograph she gave you. Can't you paint her from that?" She paused, then continued. "For that matter, couldn't you just paint all of us from looking at the photograph?"

I explained how painting from a picture is not the same as using live models. "I can do that with Avyanna," I said. "Between the photograph and the watercolor that I did of her, that should be enough. But I would prefer to paint the rest of you live if that's at all possible. It's a much better result."

"And you can't do that from the picture?" Alyssa asked. "This was Theresa's idea. The rest of us just want to get it done with as little hassle as possible."

"I understand that," I said, "but you are about to spend thousands of dollars on a custom oil painting of your family. Don't you want it to be the best quality it can be? What was the term your mother used? 'Gallery quality?' The quality of the portrait was important to her."

Alyssa smiled. "I'm sure it was. She had zero tolerance for what she considered poor workmanship." The oldest Menken sister laughed a little. "And she would tell you that. Even if it wasn't done poorly."

"She sounds like a very interesting woman," I said. "I wish I could have gotten to know her better."

"Okay, we'll go with live sittings," Alyssa said. "We'll have to set up a schedule. I'm not sure how long Jerica can stay in town. She may have to leave soon. As for the others, there shouldn't be a problem with being there." Alyssa rolled her eyes. "Destiny and Valena are the epitome of trust fund babies. They never learned how to work. Valena is apparently an 'influencer' on social media, whatever that means. Apparently, it requires large amounts of money to create the image of being sufficiently influential. Destiny doesn't even pretend to have a job. She's still *finding herself*." The eye roll that followed was almost audible.

I decided to brush over Alyssa's comments about her younger sisters and moved the conversation back to arranging for the portrait. "I'll set up a schedule," I said. "Let me know when you want me to start coming out to the house. I can't use oils here on the street and I don't have any other place where I can paint something that big."

"You mean you don't have a studio?" Alyssa asked.

I gestured towards my cart like a model on a game show. "You're looking at it. I do some painting at home, but I'm not set up for models or anything big. Not enough space, certainly not for a large canvas like what your mother had in mind. I would need to do this at your house."

"OK," Alyssa said. "I'll tell Theresa. You can use one of the guest rooms upstairs as a studio." Her voice got softer. "I didn't know it," she whispered, "but Theresa has been living in that house since the first of this year. I'm not sure why." Alyssa raised her eyebrows and cocked her head to one side. "I hope she doesn't think she's going to stay there now that Mother's gone."

That felt awkward. I didn't say anything, but it seemed that Valena and Destiny were living there as well. Or, at the very least, it was a place to put their stuff.

"Unless…" Alyssa's eyes grew wide and she let out a short gasp. "Unless Theresa knows something about the Will that the rest of us don't." She shook her head quickly and threw up her hands. "Mother was always changing her Will or threatening to change it. I think every one of us has been disinherited and eventually reinstated at one time or another. She used the threat of rewriting her Will as a way of rewarding and punishing us. We used to joke about who would be disinherited when the time came."

"Of course," Alyssa said as she sat up, "we never thought that time would actually come."

"Of course not," I said. "How could you? She was probably joking anyway."

"I wouldn't be so sure that she thought it was a joke," Alyssa said. "None of us have seen the Will. I'm not even sure who the executor is. Probably the attorney she hired instead of me. I always took care of her contracts and legal work. I still am taking care of contracts. But I guess she didn't want to put me in that position with the Will."

She cleared her throat and then went on. "We've managed to piece a few things together. She doesn't – didn't – want to sell the house to anyone outside the family, so one of us will end up with the house. We do know that much." Alyssa clenched her jaw, narrowed her eyes, and inhaled deeply. "That may be what Theresa has been trying to set up. If she's already living there, it makes sense that Mother would have given it to her. Maybe she already has, for all I know."

I sat down on my stool and wondered where this was going. "The investment portfolio can be divided up among us without too much trouble," Alyssa said. "I'm not sure how much she had in life insurance or who she had named as a beneficiary, but that money will also be coming in. The real problem is the parking lots."

Alyssa breathed a very deep sigh. "I've had the sales contracts drawn up for over a year now, but Mother refused to sign. I hope we haven't missed the window on that."

From what I'd seen, even one-fifth of the Menken fortune would be more money than most people would ever see. Certainly more than I anticipated seeing. Still, sibling rivalry had to play into this somewhere. Everybody wants to be Mother's favorite. Everyone wants a bigger piece of the pie.

"It's a lot of money and a lot of real estate," Alyssa said as she leaned towards me. "That's why I don't think this was a heart attack," she whispered. "Somebody killed our mother."

I felt simultaneously shocked and validated. And confused. "If you thought someone killed her, why didn't you say something that night? Why no autopsy to find out?"

Her face blushed with embarrassment. "I don't know. Everyone there seemed adamant about no autopsy. It made sense at the time. Now I regret the way we handled that."

"Have you talked to the police about this?" I asked.

"I did. They said they would look into it. But they're not going to spend much time on it when the death certificate says she died of natural causes."

Alyssa looked to the ground and then back up at me. "I should have backed Valena and insisted on an autopsy," she said. Then, as if she flipped a switch, Alyssa's entire face changed as she got up to leave. "I apologize. I've really said too much." She appeared more embarrassed than anything else. "I was venting. Sorry. I won't do that again."

"I promise not to say a word," I said.

"Oh," she said. "I almost forgot. This was the last thing Mother signed. Your check. We think it's because she intended to give it to you that night. I talked to the bank. You can still deposit it even though she's, well, you know... gone. The check is still good." Alyssa handed me a check for $7,500. "You're the one that solved that flute player's murder, aren't you?"

I nodded my head quickly and blinked a few times. I was shaking as I accepted the check from Alyssa. "I don't know what to say." I hugged my new patron. "Thank you."

"Thank you," she said. "Let's get this done as quickly as possible."

Then she left.

I stood there and thought about what Alyssa told me about her family and what she had to say about her mother's death. Attorneys like Alyssa Menken do not say things by accident. She wanted me to know that she thinks someone killed Avyanna. As I watched Alyssa walk away, I wondered which she wanted me to start first: The portrait or the investigation?

# Seven

I tried to absorb the conversation with Alyssa and all of its implications as I organized my paints and watched Amara performing across the street. It wasn't long before I started wondering how I could share my big news with her. It was *Nurse* day for Amara. She was working with Paul, who was dressed in his *Medic* statue outfit, to create a tribute to military medics or maybe medical people in general. I'd seen them do these poses before. Depending on the crowd, she and Paul would sometimes recruit a volunteer from the audience to be their wounded soldier patient. This meant a slight break in character for the otherwise motionless statues.

They silently waded into the audience, miming their actions and their instructions as they selected their models from the crowd. Paul's mime bordered on clownish, with exaggerated reactions and plenty of exasperation when his recruit or potential recruits didn't follow instructions or refused to play along. Amara moved more like a dancer, a graceful counterpoint to Paul's more burlesque approach.

They would eventually find their wounded soldier in the crowd. Paul would give their new partner an Army helmet and a crisp military salute, the kind that only someone who has served can pull off correctly.

I crossed the street to get closer. When Amara and Paul asked for volunteers, I made sure they saw me raise my hand. Without acknowledging that she knew me, Amara took my arm and marched me to the front of the crowd. Paul put the helmet on my head and saluted. He held it until I saluted back. He made me repeat the salute until it was done to his satisfaction.

Amara sat me down on the street with my legs stretched out in front of me. From there, she put one hand on my upper back for support and leaned me back. The pose resembled *The Pieta,* except I wasn't laying across Amara's lap. My right arm, the arm facing the audience, was raised and I was pointing to something in the distance. Once the nurse had me in position, she clicked into frozen statue mode. This was the pose, a statue of an injured soldier telling a nurse to go help her friends, the type of pose that probably, unfortunately, happened a lot in real life war zones.

"We don't have to move," I whispered. Amara did not reply or react. I thought that maybe she was thinking that I was talking about the pose. I needed to be more specific with my whispers.

I got a little louder. "We don't have to leave Pearl Street." Amara's eyes grew wide as she thought about what I said.

"They still want the portrait," I whispered again. "They gave me the check today."

"What?!" Amara screamed and dropped me. Then she picked me back up and hugged me. Everyone in the audience applauded. They must have thought it was part of the act. I jumped up, hugged Amara, saluted Paul, and ran back to my cart. Then I sent Noah a text and invited him to come over and celebrate my first big commission. I didn't say anything more. News like this should be delivered in person.

***

I was taking dinner out of the oven with the only oven mitt we owned when Noah showed up at five. That was a little early for dinner for me, but he got up at three to start muffins, donuts, and cupcakes. He was asleep by nine at the latest. I'd learned to adjust. I'd fixed red and green bell peppers stuffed with wild rice, shiitake mushrooms, and zucchini. I topped this with a sprig of parsley and a cherry tomato. I didn't cook for Noah that often, but when I did, I wanted it to look good.

"So," I put my fork down and wiped my mouth with a napkin. "Big news today." I reached across the table and took his hand in mine. "The Menken sisters want me to do that family portrait after all! Alyssa Menken gave me the first check today!" I waved the check under Noah's nose.

"I'm surprised you haven't deposited it already," he said without looking up.

"Oh, buddy, I have," I told him. "The beauty of mobile banking. Snapped a picture of it and put it in my account." I examined the check again, signed by the woman herself. The tremor in Avyanna's hand was reflected in the signature.

"I'm going to frame this," I said. "I'll hang it on the wall right over there."

"That's great." Noah said quietly. My boyfriend was, let's say, politely noncommittal about my big news. Somewhere between almost sufficiently interested and guardedly enthusiastic. Then he let go of my hand and cut into his stuffed pepper. He was still looking at the pepper when he said, "That's really great."

I was happily cutting into my dinner. "Well, I thought so." I looked at him again. "I'm going to support myself by being an artist." I gestured towards Noah with my fork to make my point. "Not only support myself, but live well. As an artist." That last part – "as an artist" – was especially important to me.

Noah had almost cleaned his plate when he asked how the house hunting was going.

"That's what's so great about the portrait!" I said. "This means Amara and I won't have to leave Boulder! We still have to find a place, but we have more options now." I left out the part about how between the canvas and other supplies, I had already spent close to a thousand dollars on this project. "This commission will pay at least five months rent in almost any place around here!"

"I'm happy you're doing the painting," Noah said. "This could open up an entirely new and potentially very affluent market." He put down his fork and cleared his throat. "I was hoping you would move in with me. There. I said it." He put his elbows on the table, leaned forward, and looked right into my eyes.

"Gabriella Alegré, would you move in with me?"

"Noah Townsend," I said in response. I took his hands in mine. I squinted at the salt and pepper shakers on the table, then at the ceiling, and finally, after a heavy sigh, back to him. "We've talked about this. I can't move in right now."

"Can't or won't?" he asked.

"Can't. Won't." I put down my fork. "I won't because I can't. Can't because I won't. Does it matter? Why are we even talking about this?"

"Because until this afternoon, you were going to need a place to live," Noah pointed out. "Because you will still need predictable income to pay the rent once this money is gone. Because I love you and I thought you loved me."

"OK," I said. "I love you. You know that, or you should by now. But moving in with someone because you have to is the worst possible reason. You move back in with your parents because you have to. You couch surf because you have to. You do not move in with your boyfriend because you have to, no matter how much you may like having his muffins for breakfast. If I move in with you, it will be because I want to, not because I plan on using you until I don't need you anymore."

"There is nothing wrong with helping out someone you care about," Noah said. "Or even helping out a friend. Why won't you let me help you?"

"Because I don't want to be helped!" My voice was perhaps slightly more emphatic than I intended but it was more restrained than it could have been. "I do not need help, at least not like that." I put my plate in the sink and moved to the couch.

"You know what I need? Supportive friends. Be that."

"You're saying you don't need, I mean want, my help because you know Gamma and Mrs. Menken were friends," Noah said from his chair at the table. Then he turned around to face me. "You're assuming I'm some rich trust fund baby who thinks he can buy himself a girlfriend." He joined me on the couch. "You would let me help you if you didn't know Gamma was rich."

I looked at Noah. "That is not true," I protested. "Are you assuming that I only want to be with you because you're rich? I also didn't want to move in with you when I thought you were just some guy working at the candy store. Until very recently, I thought you were

as broke as me." I should have known better. Loan or no loan, broke people do not go into business for themselves.

"Well," Noah cooed, "to be fair, I met you right before I quit working at the candy store." He picked up what appeared to be a boneless Miss Marple and put her on the floor. The cat meowed in protest, then raised her tail and her head and walked away.

"But," I took his hand, "even if I had known you and who you were, I still would not have wanted to move in with you. This is not about you. I don't want to move in with anyone because I don't want to move in with anyone. Why does that require any explanation?"

"You live with Amara," Noah pointed out.

"Yeah, right," I laughed. "You and I are going to live together the same way that Amara and I live together? Really? Sorry. I do not see that happening." I scooted over, picked up his arm and put it around my shoulder, and snuggled in.

"I would never sit like this with Amara," I looked up at his face. "But there is something you can do for me, as long as you're altruistically looking for things to do for people."

He sighed. "What can I do for you?"

I turned to face him and gently pushed his hair back from his forehead. "You can let me paint you. I need to practice with oil paints and I need a live model. That's the help I need right now."

"Well, you did help me decorate those cupcakes," he said.

"I did. And the cookies," I added. "Don't forget the cookies."

"And the cookies," he said, followed with an exaggerated sigh. "When did you want to start this portrait?"

I wiggled out from beneath his arm and took both of his hands in mine.

"Now," I said. "Now works for me."

Noah giggled when I led him into my bedroom. Then he tripped over my rag bucket, knocked over my trashcan, and almost fell into my easel before he hit the floor.

"Careful there," I laughed as I picked up the spilled paint-covered rags. "Is my trashcan okay?"

"It is," Noah said. "And so am I. Thanks for asking."

I showed him the stool and helped him take a seat.

Except for the bed, my bedroom looked like any other small art studio. My brushes and palette knives were laid out like surgical instruments. A stretched and primed 12x12 inch canvas was waiting on the easel. Bottles of paint thinner, mineral spirits, and linseed oil rested on a small table alongside tubes of oil paints.

"I've been practicing my oil painting," I explained. "I started practicing the day I got the commission for the portrait. Haven't stopped."

"You mean the day Mrs. Menken died," Noah said.

"Well, yes, but I thought I would frame it in a more positive light." I squeezed some burnt sienna pigment onto my palette and mixed it with a little paint thinner. "I realized that with all my other stuff, I'd let my oil painting slide. So, I started playing around with different things in here." I gestured around the room like a model on a game show.

"I've done all the classics," I said. An empty bowl sat on my dresser next to the 6x6 inch painting of that same bowl with an assortment of grapes in it. Some peaches, including one that had a bite taken out of it, were memorialized on another 12x12 inch panel. I started on an eggplant to get a feel for Destiny's hair.

I made several mistakes as I reacquainted myself with oils. Fortunately, because it takes so long to dry, oil paints can be incredibly forgiving. You can move things around and otherwise tweak mistakes much more easily than you can with faster drying paints. That was
comforting, as I considered all the possible mistakes I could make on a 72x48 inch canvas.

I was trying to decide on the color for the underpainting for the portrait. This is crucial, since the underpainting affects the tones of all the other colors in the piece. I'd tried out several, mostly earth tones. A single color 12x12 of Mrs. Menken in ultramarine blue leaned against a wall along with another just like it in burnt umber. After a few more monochromatic paintings, including some colors I blended on my own, I'd decided on burnt sienna for the underpainting of the
Menken portrait because it seemed like it worked best for the skin tones of the family.

"I'm going to use the same color underpainting on your portrait that I'm going to use for theirs," I explained to Noah. "But it's only one color. And we'll have to wait a day for the *imprimatura* to dry before I start on the final painting. I'll need you here then, too."
Noah' cheeks dimpled slightly. "*Imprimatura*," he said softly. "I love it when you speak Italian. Say it again."

I leaned in close to his left ear. *"Imprimatura,"* I whispered in my sultriest bedroom voice. Then I pulled away and went back to mixing pigment. "That's the big word for 'underpainting'. Think of it as the painting's first draft. The skeleton of the painting," I told him. "It's a thin layer of paint. But you have to be careful. If you lay it on too thick it will take too long to dry and the final picture will crack when it does." About that last part, I wasn't informing Noah as I was reminding myself. My painting of the apple was already showing signs of cracking. "Thick over thin," I said. "Thin paint first, then thicker on top."

"The *imprimatura"* – I looked over my glasses like a sexy librarian – "gives the painting more depth and definition."

"Oh yeah," he said. "More Italian. Talk to me."

"I never knew you were so into foreign tongues," I said. "Anyway, I'm going to paint your complete portrait, minus a few details, in only one color." I pointed to the three single-color portraits of Mrs. Menken. "Like those over there."

I applied the broad strokes that would be the background to get a feel for the canvas. "Some painters cover the entire canvas with that one color, like a primer coat." I picked up my brush from the canvas and turned to Noah, my accidental art student. "And that works, to an extent. I mean, it's a way to bring light into your picture, but it always felt kind of lazy to me."

I looked at my canvas. "Besides, I'll end up covering the entire canvas anyway. I'll just have more details." I dipped my brush in the burnt sienna pigment and put more paint on the canvas. "I use underpainting for contouring, shading, things like that. And to get an idea of where I want things to go."

"The painting beneath the painting," Noah said.

"Exactly. Now sit still and try not to move your mouth too much while you tell me everything you know about the Menken sisters other than how they made you wear makeup and dresses."

# Eight

I was painting yet another portrait of Amara when Theresa called.

"Your board is here!" she squealed. "Right here at my house!" Her excitement was palpable, even through the phone. "At least I think that's what it is. It's all wrapped up." She must have covered the phone with her hand but I could still hear her telling the delivery guys to take it upstairs.

"This is huge!" she kept saying. "Are you sure this is what she wanted? This is the right size?"

"That's the size she specified," I told her. "Seventy-two by forty-eight inches. Six feet by four feet. Your mother said it would be going above a couch." I thought it was interesting that Theresa said "my house" when referring to what was technically still her mother's home, or, at the very least, property of Mrs. Menken's estate. I also wondered what Alyssa, Jerica, and the sisters who also lived there would think if they heard their sister say that.

"Oh. OK. I know where she was talking about. I guess it makes sense to put it there," Theresa said. "I'm walking into that room now." She assessed the situation. "Yeah, I could see that. That works. Mother never did anything small. I had the delivery guys put it in the room you'll be painting in."

"Thanks. I wouldn't want to have to carry that up those stairs. Please don't let anyone open it or try to set it up. When would be a good time for me to come over?"

"They're setting it up now," Theresa said. She must have heard me flinch. "Was I not supposed to do that? They're putting it up on two easels I picked up last week."

I bit my lower lip and closed my eyes. People think you put a canvas on an easel and start slinging paint. I still had to put on two coats of gesso primer and then sand it smooth. I could prime on the easels, but the sanding required a more stable surface.

"Do you have a big table? Maybe a couple of sawhorses somewhere?" I asked. "If you do, have them put it on that. Or just put

it on the floor."

"I think we have some sawhorses in the garage," she said.

"I have the schedule set up for the sittings. I'm going to start with Alyssa since she's standing behind your mother. Then I'll paint your mother. I'll be using the picture and the watercolor I did for her as guides. Could you please put that in the room with the canvas?" I explained about priming the canvas and the underpainting. "Once I have the underpainting of your mother, I'll start on Jerica. Then you, then Destiny and Valena. That's the underpainting. I'll do the same schedule for the final sitting once we're through with that."

"How long should I ask Jerica to stay?" Theresa asked.

"Tell her at least a week longer, if she can," I said.

***

I explained the process again to Amara when she came home.

"Yeah, yeah, yeah." Amara threw two black jellybeans in the air and caught both of them in her mouth. "What's the plan for the investigation?"

"I'm going to interview each of the sisters as I paint their portrait, first with the underpainting and again with the final picture."

Amara shook her head. "That won't work. I know you. You don't talk when you paint. Single-syllable grunts at best."

"I'll just have to put more time between brush strokes," I told her. "Paint a little, step back and admire it, then paint a little more. Besides, I'm sure we'll have other conversations." I'd already picked up a few things from casual chats with the sisterhood, like the fact that Mrs. Menken liked to use her last Will as a way of punishing people.

"That sounds rather controlling," Amara said when I told her about the Will. "I hope you don't get that way when you get rich."

"I promise I won't," I told her. "She was also in apparently good health, or at least healthy enough to hike Trail Ridge with Theresa less than a week before she died."

*What could make a healthy woman drop dead in the bathroom?* I wondered. I remembered the tremor in her hands and the slur in her speech. Surely I wasn't the only person to pick up on that. Was that a sign?

The amateur detective in me was trying to figure out what happened to Mrs. Menken, how it happened, and, most importantly, who did it. The businesswoman in me, on the other brush, so to speak, was excited to finally be painting the picture that could introduce me to all wealthy families of Boulder and, possibly, beyond.

The artist in me just wanted to paint.

# Nine

I arrived at the Menken home precisely at eight the next morning with my toolbox, a bucket of gesso, and a three-inch paintbrush in hand, in time to see a Dr. Kurt Hickner speed walking to his Tesla S60 that was parked at one end of the circular driveway in front of the house. Neither of us acknowledged the other. Valena greeted me at the door and showed me to the room that would be my art studio for the next week to ten days.

"This was my room when I was younger," she explained. "I'm not sleeping in here now, though." The room was as big as our entire apartment, with giant windows facing the direction of the sunrise. Someone must have done some research on art studios because there were two light stands with studio-grade lights in case the sun wasn't enough. Alyssa had said this was a guest room now, but there was no bed. They must have moved it to make room for the easels and canvas. The hardwood floor and furniture were covered in drop cloths. I could rinse my brushes in the adjacent bathroom, which also had drop cloths on the floor and everything else. I wondered how messy and careless Theresa thought I must be. She wasn't taking any chances with her house.

I stepped into the space but Valena stayed back by the door. She was looking at the doorknob. "I thought she would have changed this," she said, "but I guess she never did." The doorknob locked from the hallway side instead of inside the room. You could open the door from the inside, but only if it was already unlocked from the other side. Valena smiled. "I used to sneak out after Mother was asleep. She thought she'd stop that by locking me in the room, but I figured out how to climb out the window. So she painted the windows shut." Valena turned to me. "Now you see why I don't stay in here when I come back," she said. "I've been locked in too many times."

I wanted to make sure I understood. "Your mother locked you in your bedroom?"

"She did." Valena smirked and cocked her head to one side. "On the positive side, I got the room with its own bathroom instead of having to go down the hall. Give me a fridge and a microwave and
I could have lived in here forever."

Valena looked around the room, then back to me. "There's also like zero phone reception in here. I was never sure if that was by design or if she did something to block the signal so I couldn't call my friends."

This was a side of Avyanna Menken I had not seen. "Sounds more like a timeout room than a bedroom," I said. "And you lived in here?"

"All through high school," Valena said. "Mother should have known better. She did that same thing to Jerica and you see how well that turned out. Jerica left and never came back. Mother had this incredible fear that her daughters would get in trouble and shame the family name." The potential trap of the locking door made me a little nervous, but I tried not to think too much about it. Valena's explanation made sense, even if it did seem like incredibly bad parenting. I just wouldn't close the door. It needed to be open for ventilation anyway.

The canvas rested on a large table near a wall. Above it was a very large TV screen. The easels, where I would actually be painting, were set up near another wall in the room. It wouldn't be hard to turn them around so I could see the big screen if I needed to project the picture up there.

Valena wanted to know why I only had one brush and only one bucket of paint.

"This isn't paint," I told her as I used my screwdriver and rubber mallet to pry open the lid on the bucket. "This is gesso. It's like primer for the canvas."

She made a theatrical frowning face of disappointment. "Did they send the wrong canvas?"

"Not at all," I told her. "But raw canvas like this absorbs more paint. The colors will be muted. It's the difference between a glossy finish and a matte finish. We're going for a glossier look."

Gesso is waterproof and impermeable. It prevents the oil paints from touching the actual canvas. That's important because the oils in oil paints will corrode the canvas over time.

"We had to make our own gesso at the art institute from scratch, with rabbit skin glue, acrylic paint, cornstarch, and baking soda," I said as I stirred the pre-mixed white gesso in the bucket. "Not exactly the same recipe that Rembrandt used, but close." I turned to Valena. "The instructor wanted us to experience the tradition of creating our own primers."

I looked up at Valena as I stirred. "The most important thing I learned from that experience was that tradition or not, pre-mixed gesso is a good thing."

"Here we go," I told Valena as I approached the canvas. I started painting in the center of the huge canvas, crisscrossing my strokes right, left, up, down, like the weave of a cloth. "I'll get this done, then let it dry for half an hour or so, and apply the second coat."

"Then you'll start?" Valena asked.

"Not quite. Then we'll let it sit for twenty-four hours. Then I'll sand it."

"And then you'll start," she said.

I turned to her. "Then I'll sketch the portrait in pencil. The first impression. I'll use the photograph for that." I had debated whether to sketch the entire portrait first and then start the underpainting or to skip the pencil sketch and dive right in without any guiding lines. After a few trials and many errors at home, I decided it would be safest to do the pencil sketch first. Once I had an overall first impression, then I could go into the details.

"And what is your overall first impression of our family?" Valena asked.

I suppressed a smile. "Nice pivot," I said. "I'm not sure that I had a fair first impression. That wasn't exactly a normal evening."

Valena sat down on one of the drop cloth-covered chairs. "I didn't realize it was going to be this big."

"A big family needs a big canvas." I enjoyed the feeling of painting in my new studio, even if it was only gesso and the studio was only temporary.

"Mother liked to say she had two families," Valena said. "What she really had was one family and a couple of extra kids. There wasn't
much of a sense of family at the bottom of the roster."

"Huh." I remembered Amara telling me I didn't talk while I paint. Fortunately, gesso doesn't require a great deal of concentration. I was going to have to learn to talk while painting actual images and not just backgrounds if I was going to find out what happened to Mrs. Menken.

"I'm an only child," I said. "I always wanted a sister."

"You're lucky," Valena said. "Although anything has to be better than being the 'oops' of the family. They actually called me that – Oops 2– when I was younger. Destiny was "Oops" because she popped out first. I think it was Alyssa who told them they should stop calling us that."

"That was nice of her," I said.

"Yeah," she said as she twirled her phone around in her hands. "Uncharacteristically thoughtful of her, actually. They must have had one of those anti-bullying assemblies at her school or something." Valena chuckled to herself. "But you can see how they came up with that. Just look at the age gap. Mother liked to remind us that we were proof that birth control doesn't always work."

Valena stopped talking and watched me paint. Then she picked back up again. "I never really got to know them, my older sisters, I mean. Alyssa was seventeen when we were born. She graduated from high school and left for college that same year. Never moved back into the house. I saw her a few times a year, holidays, stuff like that. Same with Theresa. I was two when she left home. She eventually came back to Boulder, after she finished college and did a few other things, so I know her a little better than I know Alyssa. But it's not like we're sisters. She's more like an aunt."

"What about Jerica?" I asked.

"Jerica," she laughed as her eyebrows went up and she shook her head. "Wow. Jerica is a whole other story. You should have heard the arguments that she and Mother would have! I was young, but I remember her being in and out of here a few times before she finally left for good. She and Mother did not get along."

Valena moved her head from side to side as her smile grew wider across her face. "That got a little better as Jerica got older, but they were never what you would call close or anything. It was not a loving relationship. I mean, they loved each other, I think. She's our mother. She had to love us, right?" Mrs. Menken's youngest daughter, or one of them, anyway, caught herself as she was speaking. "Was our mother, I meant. We have to love her. Had to love her."

I stopped painting and turned towards Valena. "She loved you. She loved each of you. I could tell by the way she talked about you when she was showing me that picture." I exaggerated a little since Mrs. Menken was no longer with us and was not in a position to contradict me.

"She may have been one of those people who have a hard time showing how they feel," I told her. What I said may have been true on some deep level, but there was a sad difference in how Mrs. Menken talked about her older daughters and the way she described her younger children.

Valena smirked. "Trust me, Mother had no trouble telling you how she felt about anything." She walked around the canvas. I could tell she wanted to touch it but, to her credit, she didn't. "It just always seemed like Destiny and I were not quite part of the group. Even now, it's like Alyssa, Theresa, and Jerica are the adults. The *successful* adults, I should add. Destiny and I are still the kids, at least where the family is concerned."

Valena sat back down. "You should hear them talk about business stuff. Destiny and I have zero input in those conversations. Alyssa wants to sell the parking lots. She keeps talking about missed opportunities and hoping it's not too late. Jerica says no, but I think she's doing it more to get to Alyssa than anything else. Theresa wanted to sell but she didn't push it like Alyssa did. It didn't matter, though.

Mother wasn't going to sell any of the parking lots."

Valena looked out the window. "That's changed now, I guess."

"Sounds complicated," I said as I put down my brush and looked at the canvas. "Now we have to let that dry for about thirty minutes and then I'll do the second coat." I sat on the stool that was there for the sisters to use when I was painting them. I wasn't sure if I should sit in the chairs, drop cloth covers or not.

"I don't know if anyone else noticed this..." Valena hesitated before she continued her thought. "I think Mother was a little drunk when she died. It was weird. She liked her martinis, but I'd never seen her when she looked like she'd had too much." Valena laughed. "I didn't think she could handle not being in complete control all the time. Guess I was wrong."

"What makes you think she was drunk?" Was Valena talking about the same tremors and the slurred speech that I saw when I painted Mrs. Menken's watercolor portrait?

"The way she was walking, her voice, all of that. I don't know if the others noticed and just haven't said anything or if I was the only one to pick up on that, but she seemed drunk to me. Not falling down, waking up with the bass player from a bar band drunk, but definitely not sober."

"You're talking about the night she, I'm sorry, died?"

"Yeah."

"Was she like that earlier that day?" I asked.

"I don't know. I was in Denver all day and didn't see her until I came up here. I don't usually hang around the house a lot." Valena stopped talking and looked down. "I'm not even sure where I'm going
to live now that Mother's gone. I was staying here, off and on. Actually, I stay in several places, depending on the evening." Valena smiled as if reflecting on her assorted temporary lodgings. "But when I'm in Boulder, I stay here. At least most of the time. I think of this as home. I'm not sure how Theresa feels about that. I know she wasn't thrilled when I showed up about a month before this reunion."

"Has Theresa told you to leave?"

"No. Not yet. But I'm sure that's coming once all this is over. I'll be on the portrait and out of the house." She walked over to the canvas again. She was being coy about it, but I could tell she wanted to touch the paint. The surest way to get someone to touch a surface is to tell them that it has wet paint.

"You don't think that's what killed her, do you?" she asked.

"Complications from having too much to drink?"

"The doctor didn't seem to think so," I said. "He said she died of natural causes."

"I guess so," she said. "I wish they'd done the autopsy so we'd know. But the others did not seem to want to do that."
I wanted to ask more questions, but Valena had already moved on to something else. She snapped a picture of the pristine white surface of the canvas lying on the table.

"Would you mind if I take pictures of this while you're working on it? My followers will love this!"

"Did the canvas feel cool?" I asked.

Valena gave me an inquisitive look. She didn't know I had been watching her hands sneaking up to get closer to the canvas.

"When you touched it just now," I teased. "It's OK. You're not going to mess anything up. Wet paint feels cool to the touch. If it didn't feel cool or sticky, then it's dry and I can start on the second coat."

"Oh." She gently touched the white gesso again. "It doesn't feel cool to me."

I picked up my brush, stirred the gesso, and started painting the second coat. Valena said goodbye and left. I guess priming a canvas isn't as exciting the second time you see it.

Jerica and Carson must have been in one of the nearby bedrooms because I heard a door close and then footsteps down the hall.

And then their muffled voices.

"Let me get this straight," Carson said. "They won't even let us see the Will for another two to three months and it probably won't be settled for six months to a year?"

"Yes, Carson." Jerica's frustration with her husband was audible. "These things are complicated."

I finished the second coat. I cleaned up everything, being extra careful not to leave gesso residue in the sink in the bathroom, and went downstairs to go home. Theresa must have seen me headed towards the front door because she called to me from the kitchen.

"All done?" she asked.

"For today. I'll come back tomorrow and sand it down to make it smooth. Then I'll sketch the outline of the entire painting. Hopefully I can get all that done tomorrow. I'll start the underpainting the next day."

"Sounds good." Theresa came closer. "What did Valena have to say? I saw her going upstairs. I started to tell her to stop, but I assumed you'd tell her to leave if you needed to work alone. She won't talk to me, so I guess I'll have to ask you what she's thinking."

"Not much," I lied.

"She's an interesting person," Theresa continued. "She has this idea that Mother was drunk the night she died."

"Was she?" I asked.

Theresa was clearly taken aback by what was admittedly a blunt question on my part. In my head, I could hear my own mom telling me that I need to learn to not be so succinct.

"She was not drunk." Theresa was adamant in defending her mother's honor. "She allowed herself one vodka martini a day, in the evenings, and that was the extent of her drinking. I was the one who made that for her. One per night. And I don't even think she'd had that evening's martini yet."

Theresa thought for a moment. "Actually, I think Carson made her martini that night. He does that when he's here."

"I'm sorry." I tried to recover from what was clearly a step over a boundary. "My grandmother is about that age and I always worry that something's going to happen to her. She's going to get sick, she's going to get hurt, something."

"It gets that way, I'm afraid," Theresa said. "We'd all like to know what happened. But even if Mother was as drunk as Valena seems to think, she wouldn't have been drunk enough to die. We would have noticed that."

"I apologize," I stammered. At this point I was hoping she wouldn't tell me to not come back. "I know how hard all this must be."

"It is hard," she said. "But not for the reasons you might think." Theresa rolled her eyes. "Family drama. It's okay. All of us are trying to figure out what happened. Sometimes there just aren't any answers."

I waited for what seemed like an appropriately long pause before I spoke. "Does eight tomorrow morning work for you? If that's too early, I can come later."

"No, that's fine. We're early risers around here." She looked down the hallway. "Well, most of us are. Valena usually sleeps until noon, when she sleeps here at all. I was surprised to see her here this morning. And who knows when or where Destiny sleeps." Theresa stopped talking. "Okay, *I'm* an early riser. Don't worry about the others."

Theresa took a seat and motioned for me to do the same. I sat down and hoped I didn't have any gesso on me that might get on the furniture. "Mother was tired of supporting Valena and Destiny. Neither one of them has ever had a real job, never tried to really do anything. Mother and I talked about how hard it is to cut off a child but how sometimes you have to do it for their own good. It's hard, but you do it. That was what Mother was going to do for them. She was going to cut off their allowance and make them fend for themselves. She wanted them to grow up."

"Did your mother cut Valena and Destiny out of the Will?"

"Who told you about the Will?" Theresa asked.

"I'm sorry," I said. "Alyssa mentioned that your mother revised her Will from time to time."

Theresa laughed softly. "Revise is a good word for that. The honest truth is we don't know. None of us have seen the Will. You would think Alyssa would have seen it, since she handled Mother's legal work, but she wouldn't even show it to Alyssa. Or at least that's what Alyssa says. We don't know who was disinherited or who was not or how anything is going to be passed along."

My host stood up. "But that Will was the only way Valena or Destiny were going to get any more of her money.

And they knew it. Mother made that abundantly clear."

# *Ten*

I decided to do one last practice sketch that night to make sure I was ready. I had sketched the photograph so many times I could do it without looking, but I still kept it pinned to my easel for reference. I was approaching the sketches as six separate portraits that happened to be on the same surface. Individuals, yet connected. Which, when I thought about it, was kind of the definition of a family. It all came down to how big did I want to make Mrs. Menken. She would determine the size of all the other figures in the painting. The photograph was taken from too far away. I wanted to zoom in. I just wasn't sure how much. With the size of this canvas, I could make this a life-sized painting. I liked that idea.

Alyssa was a potential problem. In the photo, she stood behind her mother with her hands resting on Mrs. Menken's shoulders, looking slightly downward towards Mrs. Menken. If I didn't create the right sense of depth, Alyssa and her mother would look like a totem pole.

At its most basic level, the image was a large isosceles triangle with Alyssa's face at the top and Jerica and Theresa at opposite corners, leaning slightly towards their mother. I got the impression that Mrs. Menken had said something funny and her daughters were reacting to it. Or maybe it wasn't that funny but the sisters were reacting because that was what was expected. Valena and Destiny filled in the base of the triangle and sat on the floor with their legs folded beneath them. Mrs. Menken was at the center, the all-seeing Eye of Providence in the middle of this family pyramid. I wondered if the Menken sisters would pick up on this subtle reference to the one dollar bill. After yesterday's conversations, it seemed especially appropriate.

I considered doing the underpainting in Verdaccio greens like a real Renaissance Master. Da Vinci used verdaccio when he did the *Mona Lisa,* although the Renaissance masters didn't think of it as an inside joke about the color of American currency. Verdaccio green

works really well for this kind of thing, but I wasn't completely confident in how to do something that bold. Besides, it would be the underpainting. Viewers would only see the influence of the green but not the green itself. I decided to stay with the burnt sienna that I used when I was practicing.

I had originally planned to paint Mrs. Menken first and then Jerica, since she lived so far away in Montana and would be needing to get back to her cows. But the more I thought about the pose in the photograph, the more I realized I couldn't paint Mrs. Menken until I had painted Alyssa. Alyssa stood right behind her mother. Together, they formed the centerline of the triangle. It would be easier to paint Alyssa, including the lower half of her body that was obscured from view in the photograph, and then paint Mrs. Menken over that. Trying to paint the visible portion of Alyssa's lower half around her mother would be much more difficult.

I called Alyssa. "The canvas is here," I said. "I want to paint you first and then paint your mother in front of you. I'll be sanding and sketching tomorrow, but could you come over to the house the next morning?"

"Let me check." There was a rather long pause before she came back to the phone. "You're in luck," she said. "I'm free. Weren't you over there at eight today?" she said. "Let's go with that. I'll see you then."

I realized that I hadn't painted that day. I did the gesso, but that's more like painting a wall than anything you could really call art. There was still plenty of daylight. Plenty of time to paint or draw people on Pearl Street. I picked up my things and went to my cart. I told myself I wanted to work, but actually I was avoiding the search for a new place to live. We'd had sixty days and we'd already used eight of them.

I hadn't been at my cart for long before John Spool walked over and plopped down on my stool.

"Still thinking about moving?" I asked.

"More and more," he said. "Hempy just told me he's going out of business. That means the entire building will be empty. I can either sell the place or lease it out to someone else. Honestly, I don't want to deal with leasing it."

"Hempy? The guy that sells all that stuff made of hemp?"

"That's the one," he said. "It was a good idea, but it never caught on."

"Just out of curiosity, what does a space like that lease for?"

"It leases for enough." John smiled.

Money was not a problem for John. Even if he had no money, money would not be a problem for someone like John. He's a pretty minimalist kind of guy. But John had plenty of money from Pello's life insurance and the residuals from Pello's records. The lawsuit Pello had against his former manager had been settled and John had that money, which was probably a few million. John wasn't Menken rich, but he was in a place where he could do whatever he wanted. He could live wherever he wanted. And at that time, he wanted to live near his family.

"How's the house hunting going?" he asked.

"How did you know about that?"

"Noah told me," he said. "He didn't say much about it. Just that you were going to have to move."

"He wants me to move in with him."

"Oh," John said. He voice took on a much more serious tone. "And I take it you don't want to do that?"

"I don't. Not right now, anyway," I told him. "I wish Noah understood that."

The older man patted my knee a couple of times. John's face, with all its lines and crevices, said he understood, but it was deeper than that. I felt like I had joined some club, some society of independent people.

He stood up. "Break's over. Time to get back to work."

I never understood why John was still busking. He didn't need the money. I think he just liked to perform. He had solved the introvert's dilemma, the problem of wanting to be around people and yet still be alone. Performing is a good way to get around that, a way to interact with humanity and yet maintain a safe distance.

John knew how to work a crowd and he enjoyed doing so. That was enough socialization for him. But every time he looked up, he was facing the spot across the street where Pello once played. That couldn't be easy. It could only be worse when he saw someone else there.

It was a good afternoon. I drew a woman holding her beagle puppy and a couple of random caricatures. Noah came by, which made it better.

"I told Gamma about Mrs. Menken," he said.

"How'd she take it?" I asked.

Noah picked up one of the stuffed animals I used to distract small children. "The first thing she said after I told her was 'well, I guess they can sell those parking lots now. Talk about money for nothing." Noah's eyebrows came together to create a pinched bump right above his nose. "You don't think they killed her so they could sell the parking lots, do you?" he asked.

"I don't want to think that," I said, "but look at it. That is a lot of land and a lot of money. One-fifth of that is *still* a lot. And if what they said about Mrs. Menken revising her Will and disinheriting people all the time is true, it may be divided by fewer people than that."

"I can't believe that." Noah was adamant. "I cannot picture any of those women murdering their mother. There was some tension, but not like that."

"Have you been around them recently? You're still remembering them from when you were a kid," I reminded him. "People change."

"And what about the men, their husbands?" Noah said. "Oswald and Carson? What do we know about them?"

"Not much," I said. "Other than Carson was arguing with Jerica about something. But I don't know much about any of these people." I took a long sip of coffee. "Nothing suggested Mrs. Menken was strangled. No sign of a struggle. There wasn't even any sign that she hit her head when she fell. She had a history of heart disease. If Mrs. Menken didn't die of natural causes, then what was it?"

"There was no autopsy?" Noah said, almost to himself. "No way to know for sure?"

I bit my lower lip and shook my head. "No. Her doctor didn't think it was necessary and the family did not want one. Don't get me wrong. I think she was murdered. The question is how. And who."

Noah's head dropped and his shoulders sunk. The idea that at least one of his former playmates might be a murderer seemed even harder on him than the news about Mrs. Menken's death.

After a long pause, he spoke.

"If it was intentional, then who did it?"

I took Noah's hand.

"That's what I want to find out."

# *Eleven*

I carried my sandpaper and pencils to the house the next morning. I was greeted at the door by Theresa, who waved me in without a break in her phone conversation. I headed upstairs to get to work sanding.

The gesso felt rough as I ran my fingertips across the surface. I like a little grit on surfaces when I paint, but I didn't want people to see that much texture in the final painting. There were a few bumps where I overlapped brush strokes or changed directions. I must have picked up a piece of something on my brush because there was a small clump of paint near one of the top corners. I put my mask over my nose and mouth and got to work.

I began with a sheet of coarse sandpaper to smooth out the bigger bumps then went to a finer grain for the overall sanding. Sanding by hand is one of those repetitive, mindless activities that create an almost Zen-like state of meditation. I tried to focus only on the feel of the canvas beneath the sandpaper in my hand and the sound of the sandpaper rubbing back and forth across the canvas. My mind felt clear and centered.

That peaceful feeling disappeared when Destiny entered the room wearing a loose black silk jumpsuit with lace sleeves and Doc Martin boots. Again, a much different look than the Destiny in the family photo, but I got the strong impression that this was the look and feel that Destiny preferred. Her hair was black like in the photo, but with half-inch long blonde roots. *"That explains the hat the other night,"* I thought. I made a mental note to ask Destiny if I should leave the roots in when I painted the portrait or cover them up the picture. Maybe they were part of the fashion statement she wanted to make. Same with the piercings that she had removed for the photo. I doubted that Avyanna would have wanted those in the painting.

Destiny said nothing as she sat down with her camera and started recording.

"I don't mind if you do that," I said. "But it's not going to be terribly exciting."

Destiny still said nothing. She silently recorded me as I sanded the dry gesso. She stopped recording and put her phone down after a few minutes. Her eyes were focused on the sandpaper as it moved across the canvas.

After some self-conscious sanding, I felt like I was Zenning for two.

"This will take some time," I told her as I picked up a new sheet of sandpaper. "You're welcome to stay, but it's not the most exciting part of the portrait process."

"That's fine," she said. "I've got nothing else to do." I noticed her head followed my hand when I did longer strokes with the sandpaper across the edges of the canvas. The only sound was that of the sand going across the rough canvas.

Then someone screamed.

I ran to the slightly open door with Destiny close behind, her camera already covering one eye. "That's Mother's room," Destiny whispered as she recorded. "The scream came from there." We quietly opened the door the rest of the way. Theresa was sitting on the bed, one hand over her mouth and the other holding a piece of paper.

"You okay?" I asked.

Theresa was smiling and crying at the same time. She pointed to Destiny's camera. "Could you please put that away?" She folded the paper and put it in an envelope that was beside her on the bed. "Yes, yes, I'm fine," she said. "Sorry to do that. I'm just going through Mother's things. Sometimes it's hard."

"I can imagine," I said. Theresa hugged her sister and then hugged me. Theresa was still clutching the envelope when she left the room.

Destiny and I went back to the studio. I started sanding again, but it wasn't nearly as meditative as it was before. Destiny stared at the sandpaper in my hand like a spectator at some slow-motion tennis match.

"Do you make many videos?" I asked as casually as I could.

"I record what I think is interesting," Destiny replied, her head
 still moving with the sandpaper. She permitted herself a brief smile but then it was back to the cold flat look she had when she came in. She got out her camera and started recording again.

"So you're sanding," she said after about fifteen minutes.

"Uh-huh," I said.

She put the camera down. "Removing the rough spots from the canvas that will hold our lives." Her voice was as flat as her expression. "How metaphoric."

"Uh-huh." I really needed to learn how to paint and talk at the same time.

"That's cool," she said.

"Uh-huh."

I kept sanding. When I stopped, Destiny was gone, vanished without a word. I decided to take a break for lunch before I started on the sketch.

Theresa must have read my mind. She appeared in the doorway just as I was getting ready to go get some lunch.

"I see you've met Destiny," she laughed. "I saw her coming down the stairs."

"Yeah," I said. "Not much of a conversationalist."

"No, she's really not."

"She could be one of Amara's living statues," I offered.

"Is that a real job? I'll tell her," Theresa said. "Maybe she'll stick with that one." Theresa inspected the primed and sanded canvas. "What's next?"

"Next is lunch. Then I'll start sketching the picture. It won't be as detailed as the sketches I do on Pearl Street, but you'll be able to recognize everybody. Then it will feel like we're making progress."

***

I came back after having lunch with Noah at Gamma's. Theresa helped me get the canvas off the table and up on the twin easels. I needed a stepladder to reach the top of the canvas once it was in place.

I pinned the photograph to the canvas and started the sketch using my favorite 2B pencil. It's softer and not as dark as my usual 6B that I used at my cart. If the feel of a 6B on cotton paper is almost sensuous, then the sensation of the softer 2B on canvas with sanded gesso was absolutely so. There's enough grit to pick up the pencil lead but not so much that it made the pencil bounce as I drew. I resisted the temptation to run my fingertips across the white field and focused on drawing Alyssa and Mrs. Menken.

My art instructors would have been quick to point out that what I was doing was not sketching but was instead an outline drawing, a technique I picked up from the hundreds of caricatures I'd drawn on Pearl Street. Sketching is a pretty loose way to draw, with quick, overlapping lines. It's the traditional way to start a drawing or a painting. Outline drawing uses longer, more solid lines. The drawing is defined by the shape or contours of the subject, whether it is an apple or a person. Outline drawings look cleaner than sketches. They are drawn with more precision. Not that sketches can't be beautiful. But outline drawings look, to me anyway, more like a finished product while sketches often look as though they are waiting for the next step in a bigger process. A caricature is basically a line drawing with just enough detail to make it personal.

Six months of drawing caricatures had made me quite proficient at outline drawing. First, you identify the basic shapes in the subject. For the Menken portrait, the overall shape was a triangle. On the sides were the slight curves. There were other curves, circles, and arcs throughout the image. There were no squares or sharp corners at all.

Nothing about art is mindless, but there are some steps in the process that allow for more mind wandering than others. Applying gesso and sanding are good examples of that kind of thing, although my potentially mindful gesso sessions had been interrupted by visits from Valena and Destiny. I found my mind returning to those conversations as I drew the basic shapes of the portrait.

How would it feel to be the younger sister of such successful women with such strong personalities? And to know you were one of
the "oops" sisters?

I wondered if anyone ever pointed out the strong possibility that any one of the sisters, even all of them, could very well have been unintended. And yet, the name was only given to the twins. I couldn't imagine Alyssa's reaction if someone referred to her as an "oops." Valena said that it was Alyssa who ultimately stood up for her and her sister and told the family to stop calling them that. Did Alyssa realize that she could very well be an oops herself?

The outline drawing of Jerica's long curls proved to be more challenging than the totem pole of Alyssa and Mrs. Menken. I found myself moving away from capturing the overall shapes and getting caught up in the details of her hair. I stepped back, refocused, and moved to Theresa's side of the canvas.

I squatted down to draw the twins but still had a hard time reaching Valena and Destiny at the bottom of the expanse. That was fine for this drawing, but I knew I would have to raise the canvas for their parts of the painting. I wasn't sure if the easels could extend that high or if they would support the canvas if they did. But if I was going to give Destiny and Valena the attention they deserved, I need to lift them up as high as their sisters were when I drew them. I suspected that kind of equality was not often the case off the canvas.

I was so involved with the drawing that I did not hear Theresa coming up the stairs.

"Oh my," she said. "I like that. It's a nice clean look. You could almost do a portrait with nothing but lines." She walked closer to the canvas. "And now you'll color all this in?"

"It's not quite that simple, but, yeah. Now I color it in. Twice." I checked the time. I did not realize it was so late.

"And I will start that tomorrow with Alyssa."

# *Twelve*

My Uber dropped me off the next morning in time to watch Alyssa get out of her car and walk across the wide circular driveway to the house just as Dr. Hickner's car was pulling into the street. Alyssa and I had not discussed what to wear, but she was wearing the same outfit she wore in the original photo. I hoped all the sisters would make that same wardrobe choice. I felt confident about Theresa and Valena. I had no idea what Jerica might wear. Or Destiny.

I followed Alyssa as she marched straight into the house without touching the doorbell or even saying hello. Theresa jumped when the door opened. Valena even looked up from her phone. I hesitated before going in, but then followed in Alyssa's footsteps.

"Sorry," I said. "Excuse me."

"Theresa, did we catch you at a bad time?" Alyssa laughed. "Valena, could you be a dear and go get me a glass of grapefruit juice and bring it upstairs for me? Thank you."

Without a word, Valena dutifully got up and went to the kitchen. Alyssa and I went upstairs to work on the portrait.

Alyssa raised one eyebrow as she looked around the room. "I see Theresa has made some changes. I guess she needed an office, so she took over the guest room." She said nothing about the outline drawing. She ran her hand across a clean part of the canvas then rubbed her fingers with her thumb.

"Did you sand this?"

I chose to ignore that. "Your mother said you were an attorney," I said as I was setting up. "That must be an interesting job."

"It's not as interesting as you might think," she said. Alyssa checked the time on her phone and watched as I used my palette knife to mix burnt sienna pigment with mineral spirits. Mineral spirits work best for pigments in underpaintings. I would use linseed oil as the medium for the final picture. I mixed the paint until it was almost the consistency of watercolors.

"Are we going to get started soon?" Alyssa asked. "I have to be somewhere at ten."

I picked up my brush. "Starting right now." I looked at the clock. "I'll do your face first. I can do the rest from the picture if you have to leave."

I had been watching instructional videos about painting, not because I needed to learn how to paint but because I needed to learn how to paint while carrying on a conversation. The painters online talk the entire time they're painting. Of course, that's scripted and they know what they're going to say before they start. And they're not listening to anyone while they're working. It's not a conversation. But they are talking with entire words and complete sentences. There is a certain rhythm to it. That's what I needed to learn.

"Remember," I said to Alyssa, "this is the first coat. It will be in one color and not as highly detailed as the final painting."
"Right, right," she said impatiently. "The underpainting. I took art appreciation in college."

I raised my brush and applied the first stroke of paint to the beautifully smooth white canvas I had worked so hard to prepare. It felt like the first kiss in a new relationship.

Valena brought in Alyssa's juice. Alyssa took the glass and held up one finger, an unspoken command for Valena to wait. She drank the entire glass without putting it down while Valena stood there waiting. She gave the glass back to Valena when it was empty.

"Try to smile," Valena said as she walked out the door.

"That girl," Alyssa said, shaking her head. "Valena needs to get her life together, get a job, and start acting like an adult. She is always, was always, asking Mother for money. And Mother simply gave it to her, along with her regular allowance. There's no telling how much money she's taken over the years. It's no wonder she never does anything. She doesn't have to." Alyssa smoothed her dress around her hips. "I'm sure she'll burn through her share of the estate in no time and will be asking the rest of us for help." The tall brunette turned to me. "I know everyone thinks we have all this money. And we do. But trust me, a million dollars doesn't go as far as it used to."

Jerica strode into the room, took off her baseball cap, and dropped into the chair by the door. "No, it doesn't," she said. "But a hundred million would go one hundred times further."

Alyssa spun to face Jerica. I stopped painting. My reflex was to ask her to sit still and try not to move when she spoke. Alyssa Menken did not seem like the kind of woman who took orders from others. Her demeanor reminded me of the brief encounter I had with her mother.

"Come on, Alyssa," Jerica said as she picked at something on the bottom of one of her boots. "It's no great secret that Mother had money. I'm sure Gabriella knows that. If she didn't before, then she's probably figured it out by now." Jerica looked at me. "Honestly, I have no idea how much Mother's estate is worth. Alyssa may, since she handled Mother's legal stuff. Well, most of it, huh Alyssa?" Jerica chuckled then winked at me.

"Mother wouldn't let her attorney daughter handle the Will," Jerica told me in a stage whisper. "Alyssa doesn't like to talk about it."

The oldest Menken daughter turned and glared at the middle child again.

"Why are you doing this?"

"I'm sorry," Jerica said to her sister. "Which is more embarrassing for you? That you're rich and didn't earn it or that Mother didn't trust you to handle her estate?" Jerica kept on talking to me. "We don't know how much she was worth. I'm not sure anyone does on any given day, the way markets and land values fluctuate these days. We don't know how it will be divided in the Will. But it is safe to assume that each of us will get several million dollars. A few hundred million each is not out of the question. Possibly more. That's hardly news to anyone."

Alyssa did not break her pose as she spoke. "And I'm sure Jerica will donate all of hers to some worthwhile organization."

"I may," Jerica said. "I haven't decided what I'm going to do with it, honestly." She smiled at her sister. "I've done fine without it so far, unlike the rest of you."

Alyssa took a deep breath, closed her eyes, and raised her chin a little higher, completely changing the contour of the line I was painting. I pulled back from my canvas and tried to hide my frustration with the distractions.

"Could you please go back like you were?" I asked Alyssa.

"Oh. Yes," said my model. "Sorry."

Jerica stood up to leave. "When did you want to paint me?"

I stopped painting while I thought about schedules and logistics. "I'll get Alyssa and your mother done today. Want to come in tomorrow at eight?"

"See you then." Jerica waved goodbye to Alyssa. "Later, sis."

Alyssa ground her teeth and inhaled deeply as Jerica left the room but was careful not to move her head. "Jerica may not know it, but the final version of the Will might not matter at all," she said. "Mother wasn't exactly herself those last few days. We may have to challenge the latest version if it is too recent or if it looks like she was unduly influenced by someone. That could get ugly, but it's important to do what she would have wanted and not to do something that she wouldn't have done had she been of sound mind."

There's no point in trying to paint an angry face. I asked Alyssa if she wanted to take a break.

"That sounds like a good idea," she said. Alyssa dropped into the chair. "I didn't know being still could be so tiring. How does your friend do that all day?"

"I have no idea," I laughed. "But, if it's any consolation, your pose is a lot easier than Jerica's or Theresa's. Look at the angle of their heads in that photograph."

Alyssa took the photograph off the clip and looked at it. "That's what they get for not looking at the camera." She sat back down.

"Our parents had money and they used it to help their daughters," she said in a very matter-of-fact voice.

"Except Jerica," I guessed.

"Exactly," Alyssa said. "Jerica left home before she even graduated from high school. She made it very clear that she did not want their money, did not need their help, and did not want to be a part of this family. They made up eventually. Jerica started coming home for Christmas, things like that. But there was always a distance there."

"That's too bad," I said. "Still, she seems like a nice person."

"Ha!" Alyssa smiled. "Doesn't she, though? Simple farm girl. Rancher's wife. What a setup. I hope she's happy because I know she isn't rich."

I weighed my next words carefully before I said them. I didn't want to bring up bad memories.

"She certainly did her best to save your mother," I said.

I was relieved when Alyssa nodded her head in agreement. "Yes, she did." Her voice had more than a touch of sisterly admiration. "That was pure Jerica. Decisive, take charge, and pure physical strength. She's always been that way."

I stirred my paint and carefully added more paint thinner. "Did they make that same offer about college to Destiny or Valena?"

"Of course," Alyssa said. "Why wouldn't they? But that money didn't come without some strings attached, at least not for the three of us. Our parents gave all of us an allowance. All the clichés are true. But they made it very clear that allowance would end if we dropped out of school." She laughed. "They didn't follow up on that, but that was their original intent."

Alyssa chuckled to herself. "That attitude of giving us money with strings attached eventually evolved into Mother threatening to disinherit us when she was angry." Alyssa made sure I was looking at her. "That's why she wouldn't let me see the Will. She didn't want me to know whether I had been disinherited. And I'll admit it. I can't speak for Theresa, but that's why I went on to law school. My parents were paying tuition. They were giving me an allowance. Why wouldn't I stay in school, especially since I wanted to be a lawyer anyway?"

Alyssa stood up and stretched as if she was about to run a marathon. "They told me the allowance would end when I finished law school, but they didn't. I still receive the same allowance that I did in college. They even adjusted it for inflation!

But I don't use it to live on like the twins do or as a slush fund for incredible vacations like Theresa." She started doing neck rolls. "Mother said she didn't want to punish me for being successful. That
she was proud of my initiative and hard work."

Alyssa turned to me. "She should be," she added.

"I set all that money aside in separate accounts," Alyssa said. "And I act as if it isn't there. I've put every penny of it into a college fund for my kids." I couldn't tell if the pride in her voice was because she'd saved all that money or because she was proud of her children. "There's enough in there now for both of them to get multiple Ivy League PhD's, if that's what they want to do, without me having to tap into any other funds. I told Mother what I was doing and she approved."

She put the picture back on the clip and faced me. "I guess I am like Jerica in that respect. I wanted to prove that I could make it on my own without their money." She allowed herself a self-satisfied smile. "And now I have my own law firm with four partners. And I did that on my own."

I was stirring paint as slowly as the laws of physics and viscosity would allow. "I'm sure your parents were very proud of you."

Alyssa stood facing herself in the mirror. She grabbed one foot and raised the other over her head. "They were, even if Mother could never bring herself to say it. But apparently the rules were different for the Oops family back there. Their allowance kept coming even when they didn't go to college, even when they didn't start their own businesses. They didn't have to show any initiative or any effort towards anything at all. At least Jerica has done that much with her cows."

Alyssa changed poses and kept stretching. "And those are *her* cows." She emphasized the feminine pronoun. "People assume that since Carson is a man, he already had that all set up and Jerica just married into it. It's exactly the opposite. Jerica built that ranch, that business, on her own. She'd been in the cow business for years before
she met Carson. Carson brought his experience of growing up on a ranch but nothing else of any value. At least not that I can tell."

She put her hands on her hips and swiveled back and forth as she watched her reflection in the full-length mirror on the other side of the room. "Jerica actually has a degree in business that she picked up at some state school somewhere along the way. That's where she met Carson. In a college business class."

I pointed to the canvas with my brush. "Are you ready?"

"Sure." My model stepped back into position but kept on talking. "Valena was trying to tell me what being a social media influencer is and how people make millions of dollars from that. More power to her. I don't get it. And if it requires work, then I especially don't see it working for her. But maybe I'm wrong."

"Why do you say that," I asked.

"Because," Alyssa smirked. "She's never stuck with anything long enough for anyone to know. Besides, that would require planning. Valena couldn't develop a plan for anything."

I finished the underpainting of Alyssa. "Your mother will go there," I pointed. "Just like in the picture."

"Why don't I have any hands?"

I laughed. "I'll paint those when I paint your mother. They'll be on her shoulders, just like in the picture."

"Be sure they're on her shoulders," she said. "Everyone around here thinks I would rather have them around her neck."

# Thirteen

I finished up Alyssa and Mrs. Menken that morning. I decided to spend my free afternoon on Pearl Street, sitting at my cart, drawing complete strangers, and listening to the musical stylings of Mr. John Spool. Maybe go by Noah's and get a cupcake. Pearl Street wasn't just where Amara and I worked. It was our home, in many ways more so than our actual address.

I was preparing myself for the likelihood that Amara and I could be leaving Pearl Street. Maybe leaving Boulder altogether if we couldn't find a place to live. Maybe even leaving one another, if things really got bad. My mother would have said that it was time to buckle down and get a real job, which is why I had not told her about my current housing crisis. I'd heard enough about how art could not be a real job when I was growing up. But I wondered if this might prove that she was right.

The street was busy with foot traffic. I did a couple of quick caricatures within the first half hour I was there. It felt good to do some fun, low-pressure line drawings. Then I took a break and walked down to listen to John singing his blues songs. There, reclining on the grass beside the street, was Destiny Menken, fully decked out in all her darkness with the addition of a massive silver cross suspended by a silver chain above the plunging neckline of her black dress.

"You're a fan of John Spool?" I said.

"Yeah," the goth sister said and momentarily lowered her camera. "You?"

I smiled. "He's a friend of mine."

We sat for a while and listened to the music without saying anything. Destiny recorded more of John. It was a pleasant, relaxing afternoon on the grassy lawn off the sidewalk.

Destiny moved closer to me and spoke softly. "You think one of us killed Mother. That's what you're doing, right? An investigation?"

I was surprised to hear Destiny speaking so freely. Up to that time, that was one of the longer thoughts I had heard Destiny express. I kept watching and listening to John, hoping not to break the conversational mood. "I'm painting a family portrait," I told her as I smiled with my entire face. "That's what I do."

"Right," Destiny went back behind her camera.

I wasn't sure what to say. Alyssa was the one who asked me to look into her mother's death. Had she told the others? And why would she do that if she knew that one of them was the killer? I needed to know how much Destiny knew and how she came to know it.

"I'm an artist," I repeated. "Your sister asked me to do the portrait your mother ordered. That's all I'm doing. Painting a portrait. And keeping a promise."

"Well, that's disappointing." Destiny put the camera on the ground. "I was hoping someone would care enough to do something."

She sounded sincere. She sounded hurt. And she sounded like she knew something.

"My money's on Alyssa," she said without me asking anything. "She's the one you have to watch. Alyssa is the one who convinced Mother to cut off our allowance. Alyssa is the one who was really pushing her to sell those parking lots." She pulled her knees up to her chin, creating a small black ball. "Alyssa is all about the money. That's Alyssa."

I almost told Destiny that Alyssa was the one who asked me to investigate, but I stopped before I did.

"I don't need the money," Destiny continued. "This dress? Goodwill. This necklace? The Arc. This entire outfit was less than twenty dollars." She smirked. "That's what they don't get. It's not about money. It's about creating an individual style." She picked up her camera and started recording John as he sang. "John's got style. That's why people love him." She was right about John.

"And those boots?" I couldn't help asking.

Destiny put down her camera when John finished his song. "Okay, these boots *were* expensive."

She grinned and ran her fingertips along the top of one boot. "But it's not like I had to kill somebody to get the money."

"It has to be Alyssa," she repeated. "All Theresa cares about is the house and Jerica is even more anti-money than I am."

I kept asking myself if this the same woman who barely said anything when she was watching me prime that canvas.

"What about Valena?" I asked. "Does Valena care about money?"

"Ha!" Destiny's laugh exploded. She snickered as she talked about her twin. "She certainly did after Mother told us she was going to cut us off. She won't have to worry about it now."

Destiny turned to me. "Our allowance showed up in our checking accounts on the first day of the month." She stopped as she processed what she had said and suddenly seemed very anxious. "Do you think that will still happen? How does that even work when someone, you know, dies?"

"I have no idea," I told her.

"Doesn't matter," she shrugged. Destiny tugged at her dress. "Goodwill, eight dollars. I save the rest. It's like a scorecard in my own personal game." She looked at me. "Valena says I'm hoarding money, as if that's a bad thing."

"My friend Amara bought a wedding gown there," I told her. "I don't know what she paid, but it couldn't have been much. Amara gets most of her costumes there. There and The Arc." I'd always wondered about the gown Amara wore for her *Bride Throwing Her Bouquet* statue. It reminded me of the famous six-word Hemingway story. "For sale: Wedding gown. Never worn." Except Hemingway's story was about baby shoes. Same idea.

"Great stuff. You should try it out." Destiny leaned back with her hands on the grass. "Alyssa believes that the city is going to use eminent domain to take the parking lots so developers can build cheap apartments near downtown Denver."

"Eminent domain," I repeated. I was impressed with Destiny's use of the legal term. "They can do that?"

"Kelo vs. City of New London." Destiny cited the case with no effort at all. "2005. In a four-five decision, the Supreme Court of the United States ruled that the government could take privately-owned land and turn it over to a private developer for commercial purposes if it provides necessary economic growth for the community." She turned to me. "They could decide that Denver needs crappy housing in ugly buildings more than it needs expensive parking."

I was impressed. "I thought Alyssa was the only attorney in the family."

"Only because I chose not to go to law school." She brushed something off of the bottom of her dress. "The city would have to pay fair market value, but they'll lowball it. Alyssa thinks we should sell while we can and get as much as we can before that happens."

"She may have a point," I said.

"Not really. Everyone thinks Alyssa is the smart one," Destiny said, "but she's really not that bright. She's a hardworking overachiever who looks good in a business suit. I wouldn't simply accept everything she says as fact. Besides, Mother did not want to sell the parking lots and she shouldn't have to explain that to anyone. Maybe it's some sentimental attachment to Dad. I don't know."

"Sentimental attachments can mean a lot," I said. "It's hard to give up the things that remind us of someone we love."

"Or maybe she thinks she can get more for it in the future." Destiny rolled her neck and looked at me. "The entire system is fueled by the interaction of greed and fear, right? It's like the balance of sodium and potassium that keeps your heart beating. Maybe Mother was greedy for more money and Alyssa is afraid of a market collapse."

"What do you think?" I was fascinated by the suddenly articulate and knowledgeable woman sitting beside me. Talk about don't judge a book by its cover. "Should she have sold the parking lots?"

Destiny looked at the increasingly black silhouette of the Flatirons at sunset and then back at me. Then she floored me with her analysis.

"No," she said. "Mother was right not to sell. Denver, for that
matter the entire State of Colorado, lacks the public transportation infrastructure necessary to support a car-free city, even with a high-density population living in high-rise buildings that combine residential, retail, and office space. No. You will always have people driving in from places like Boulder or the mountains. Until they can build that infrastructure and can convince our car-oriented population to give up personal transportation and use mass transit, people are going to need somewhere to park their cars."

I was floored, not by the wonky technocrat language, although that was certainly impressive, but by how much more verbal Destiny was when she was away from her sisters. I'd heard about selective mutism. Was Destiny unable to talk around her sisters? What causes something like that?

Destiny was not finished. "My mother was murdered by someone in that house. The doctor should have done his job and ordered an autopsy. He didn't. The police should have looked into it. They didn't."

She stood up to leave. "I want to know what happened to my mother. Are you going to help me or not?"

# Fourteen

That night, I dreamed Amara and I were looking for somewhere to live. We were going door to door asking people if they had any rooms for rent. We ended up sleeping on the sidewalk beside my cart where we were yelled at by Alyssa Menken for violating the city camping ordinance. I woke up in a cold sweat.

I hated to admit it, but I was seriously thinking of moving in with Noah for all the wrong reasons. Rentals wanted the first and last month's rent to move in, plus a deposit on top of that. And our deposit would be even higher because we had a cat. Basically three months rent all at once. My $7,500 suddenly didn't seem like that much. It could get us in a place, maybe, somewhere, but it wasn't going to last and it probably wouldn't get us utilities. Granted, I still had the other half coming when I finished the picture. And neither one of us was going to quit working. There would still be income. I just wasn't sure it would be enough.

I told Amara about my dream as we walked to Noah's for coffee before I had to be at Menken Manor. "I suppose we could buy sleeping bags and sleep behind my cart," I said.

"I'm pretty sure the city of Boulder has some law against camping on the sidewalk," she said. "Besides, where would we change clothes?"

"And where would Paul sleep?" I teased. I wondered if Paul made Amara the same offer about moving in that Noah made to me. Somehow, I didn't think so. I wasn't even sure Paul was in the position to extend that kind of invitation. For all I knew, he might have been living with his parents. But if he had asked her to move in with him, I knew Amara would have the same reaction I had. The only thing stronger than Amara's sense of independence was her complete lack of concern for what others thought of her choices.

I thought about calling Theresa and telling her I couldn't come over because I had to look for a place to live. Amara must have read my mind.

"Let's do this," she said. "You go to the Menken's like you planned. I'll spend the day looking around to see what I can find. What good is being self-employed if you can't take the occasional day off?"

"That's great," I said, "except we've checked out every available place around here."

Amara didn't seem too concerned. "New places open up all the time," she said. "It's getting close to the end of the month. People will soon be moving or telling their landlord that they're going to move. New places will open up. You'll see."

"It really doesn't matter if they're open if we can't afford to move in," I said as I opened the door to Gamma's Cupcakes. "Not a word of this to Noah, OK?"

"I wasn't the one who gave it away last time," Amara reminded me and laughed. "I promise, I will not say anything to Noah."

"Middle finger swear?" I said.

"Middle finger swear," she echoed and laughed. We decided that pinky swears were too cliché long before this.

As usual, Noah came out from behind the counter to greet us with a coffee cup in each hand.

"How's it going?" he asked.

"The painting?" I asked. "Great! I finished up the first coat of Alyssa and her mother yesterday. Today I'm going to do Jerica and Theresa."

"Not what I meant," he said, "but thanks for that update."

"Oh, I'm sorry. The investigation? Kind of slow. I have some ideas, but no proof. It is an interesting family, I'll say that."

"Again," he said, "not what I meant. But also good to know."

"Oh," I said, pretending I had suddenly figured out what he must have been talking about. "The search for affordable housing? The quest continues."

"My offer still stands." Noah turned to Amara. "Sorry. I only have room for one."

Amara waved her hand and said nothing.

"She's taken a vow of silence," I explained. "Celibacy is next." Amara almost spit her coffee across the table when she heard that.

"And then poverty?" Noah said as he handed Amara a napkin and pointed to his own chin. "Right there. Got it."

"Already there, rich boy." I saw Noah's reaction and immediately regretted what I had said.

"I didn't mean that, I'm sorry."

"No. I get it," Noah said. "I think I have cupcakes to bake or something to do back there. Amara, have a great day."

"What was that?" Amara scolded me before Noah even made it back to the counter. "It's not his fault he was born into a rich family."

"I know," I said. "It's just... It's the Menken sisters. You can see what money did to that family. They all hate each other, except Valena and Destiny. They seem to get along. But only with each other."

"Sounds like they had to," Amara reminded me. "Their older sisters sound pretty intimidating. And what's up with Jerica?"

"Jerica is different," I said. "She walked away from all that." I thought about the conversations I'd overhead that first night and since I'd been in the house. "But they must be having money problems, Jerica and Carson. I don't know the specifics. But apparently Carson wanted to ask Mrs. Menken for some money. Actually, he wanted Jerica to ask her. Maybe a loan or something."

"And she died before he could ask? Or before Jerica could?" Amara asked.

"Yes," I said between sips of coffee. "But Jerica wouldn't ask her. And she wouldn't let Carson ask her, but Carson was threatening to ask her anyway. That's what he and Jerica were arguing about when I heard them the night Mrs. Menken died."

"And that rules them out as suspects," Amara said. "Even though I thought Carson was kind of sketchy."

"I know," I said. "I'm not sure what it is, but he rates very high on the creep-o-meter. A cowboy with a haircut like that? And dressed like that? I mean, I know he wasn't working, but still. When you look at Jerica, what do you see?"

Amara smiled. "Cowgirl. She is pure cowgirl. I don't know how she got there coming from that family, but that's what she is."

"Exactly," I said. "I could see her riding a horse while she lassoes a calf and wrestles it to the ground or whatever they do after they lasso a calf. And strong. You should have seen how she pushed her sister out of the way the other night to do CPR." Jerica had the physical strength that comes from hard work, the kind of work you would do on a ranch. She had the attitude of someone who was proud of her independence and her accomplishments.

I looked at Amara. "Do you see any of that in Carson?"

"Well," she said. "I didn't really talk to him. I don't know."

"You didn't see it because it's not there." I leaned closer to Amara. "I saw a man telling his wife to go against what she has rejected since she was in high school, to go against her sense of who she is, and to beg her mother for money. I can't imagine how hard that must be for someone like Jerica. No wonder she wouldn't do it."

"You can imagine it because you're the same way," Amara said.

"Maybe that's why I like Jerica so much," I said.

"And Carson's a jerk and a grifter," Amara said. She picked up her coffee but put it back down without drinking any. "That doesn't make him a murderer," she said. "If anything, that rules him out as a suspect. He wouldn't kill his mother-in-law if he thought there was a chance she might give them some money."

"Maybe," I said. "But why ask for a loan when you can get an inheritance?"

Amara sat back in her chair and shook her head. "Why would he ask Jerica to talk to her mother about a loan if he was going to kill her?"

"Because it makes a better alibi."

***

I left the cupcake shop in time to keep my appointment with Jerica at the Menken house. She met me at the door. I was glad to see she was wearing the same clothes she had on in the picture.

"I love your hair," I confessed as I was setting up and getting ready to paint.

"Thanks. Trust me, it only looks like this when I'm here," she said. "Most of the time I shove it under a hat. Valena does it for me when I'm in town."

"Valena does hair?" I wondered what she could do for my curls.

"Not professionally or anything." Jerica laughed. "I'm not sure how Mother would have felt about having a hairdresser in the family." Jerica imitated her mother's voice as she looked in the mirror. "It's so subservient." She kept talking as she studied the photograph for her pose. "Although, towards the end, Mother probably would have been happy to see Valena doing anything. But, to be fair, Valena is talented like that. She can do wonders with makeup. She did all of us that day. It was kind of fun, actually. A big makeup party. Felt like I was a kid again."

"Apparently she and Destiny did the same thing to my boyfriend when they were kids," I said.

"Oh! That's right!" Jerica spun around as she leaned her head back and laughed. "You're friends with Noah Townsend! Mother mentioned that. He was such a cute little kid! He reminds me of me."

"How so?" I asked.

"Not the cute part," she said. "He's much cuter than me. The part where he walked away from the whole rich family thing, although I think Mother said that his grandmother co-signed a loan for him so he could buy that store."

"Bakery," I said. "It's a bakery. He sells cupcakes, muffins, things like that."

"Right. A cupcake place. That was it. I mean, Julia could have bought that building without even noticing the price, but Noah wouldn't borrow the money from his grandmother, much less take it as a gift. She's just a cosigner on the business loan." The Menken's middle child paused for a brief moment before she spoke again. "And, if we're being completely honest, my parents did the same for me. That's how I started the ranch. They cosigned and I'm making the
payments. I am still making the payments. The others don't know that."

*That explains how she got her start,* I thought.

We were about to get started when Destiny walked into the room with half of her face behind the camera.

"Mind if I record this?" she asked.

"I don't mind," I told her.

"What is this?" Jerica said. "'Meet the Menkens?' I feel like I'm part of a reality show. And why don't you use your phone instead of that huge camera?"

Destiny moved the camera away from her face. "This huge camera makes you look better."

"In that case," Jerica laughed, "use the camera. Did you know that our artist here is a friend of Noah Townsend's?"

Destiny kept recording. "Really?" she snickered. "A good friend?" She kept the camera on Jerica as she circled around the room.

"Does Noah ever talk about his parents?" Jerica asked me.

"Not really," I said.

"I wouldn't think so," Jerica said. "They had this big fight when he told them he wanted to make it on his own. They wouldn't mind him owning his own business. They didn't want him to actually work at it. That's what employees are for."

"His grandmother seems to love him," I countered.

"She does," Jerica continued. "She also understands hard work and what it means to build a business. His parents – both of them – grew up after his grandparents had done all the work. Noah's parents don't know what it means to build anything."

What Jerica said did put some things into perspective. "We've been together almost six months now. I didn't know he was rich until I met your mother."

"And if he's like me," Jerica said, "that's exactly how he wanted it. And, to be fair, he may not be rich. He may not have any money at all. I'm not sure what kind of trust fund or other arrangements his parents made. But he doesn't seem to live like he is."

"No, he doesn't," I said, as I fell in love with my boyfriend all
over again.

"I remember when Carson found out about my family," Jerica said quietly. "Things changed. It's been different since he found out."

We were both silent for a while. I painted and thought about Noah. Destiny kept recording her video. I assumed Jerica was thinking about Carson because she did not look as happy as she did in the photograph. I softened up her jaw and opened up her eyes a bit on the canvas. Good thing this wasn't going to be the final painting. I painted for about fifteen minutes and then asked her if she wanted a break. Fifteen minutes is about all a model can take. After that, they get fidgety and need to move.

"Yes!" she said. "I never knew standing still could be so hard." She looked in the mirror again. "I should have had Valena do my makeup," she said.

"Not today," I said. "This is all just blocking out contours and shapes. You may want to do more makeup for the final picture, but you really don't have to do it then, either. I can work wonders with a paintbrush."

Destiny must not have felt like socializing. "Let me know when there's something interesting."

Jerica was very quiet. "She's upset about Mother dying."

"That's very understandable," I said. "Anyone would be."

"Yeah, but she seems to be taking it harder than the rest of us," Jerica said. "I wonder how Valena feels right now. I mean, she's sad just like the rest of us. But... well... Mother told her she was going to stop her allowance. No tapering off, no trial period. Just a hard stop. Same for Destiny. That's all changed now, I guess."

"Your mother told you this?" I asked.

"Valena told me this. She thought I would understand, I guess." Jerica shrugged. "Of course, I didn't understand, at least not like Valena expected. I mean, yes I understood and I agreed with Mother. What I didn't understand – don't understand – is why Mother
let it go on for as long as she did."

"And your mother gave that same message to Destiny?"

"Yes," Jerica said. "At least that's what Valena told me. But

Destiny is different. I mean, she has the same allowance as Valena. But money doesn't seem to be as important to her. Valena is all about image, and that image is expensive to keep up. Destiny could care less. She'll take the money if it's there, but she would probably be okay if it wasn't. Or at least she thinks she would. She might have been in for a surprise if it had stopped, but she didn't seem to be worried about it." She thought about that for a second. "Destiny misses Mother. Valena is afraid she'll miss the money."

Jerica looked out the windows. "But they won't have to worry about that now, I guess. They're going to get hundreds of millions of dollars just like the rest of us, as long as Mother didn't disinherit them." She laughed and turned towards me. "Honestly, I think that whole disinherit thing was just one of her jokes. I don't think she'd actually do that. She told me I was in the Will even after I told her I didn't want to be." Jerica got up to get back in position so I could continue. "I still haven't decided what I'm going to do with it. Carson thinks we should sell the ranch and retire while we're still young enough to enjoy it, but I don't want to do that. I already enjoy what I do. I love that it's mine."

She broke her pose and turned to me.

"If I am in the Will, I'll probably give the money away to some charity. Several charities. Maybe start a foundation for young women who want to go into business or something.

"What does Carson think about that?" I asked.

Jerica looked at the canvas and the single-color paintings of her sister and her mother.

"It's not his money," she said very matter-of-factly.

***

I was almost finished painting Jerica when Valena walked in to see how things were going.

"You should have let me do your makeup," she said to her sister. Do you want me to do your hair before you pose for the final painting of this?" "Sure," Jerica said to her sister. "Is Carson up yet? You can tell he's on vacation, although this hasn't turned out to be much of a vacation, has it?"

"No, it hasn't," Valena said, then she shifted gears. "Carson and Theresa are in the kitchen making some coffee or something. I can check and tell him to come up here if you want."

"No," Jerica laughed. "I don't need him up here. But, if they're making coffee, could you be a dear and go me get some? And bring one for Gabriella, too. Thanks."

Valena came back in a few minutes with two coffee mugs. "Guests first," she said as she handed one of them to me. Jerica's mouth twisted into a half smile as she watched Valena hand the mug to me. Valena smiled like a homecoming queen as she looked at her sister.

"Oops," Valena teased. "Sorry, Jerica. I forgot that's your special mug."

"Right," Jerica said. "Be a dear and go ask Mr. Barista down there what he plans to do for lunch, would you?"

"What was that about?" I asked after Valena had left.

"Nothing," Jerica said. "I gave that mug to Mother a few years ago. I've been drinking out of it ever since, well, you know. Since we got here. It's not a big deal."

I felt guilty but it really wasn't my fault. I took the mug I was handed. "I could give it to you but I've already drank out of it."

"No, that's fine." She set the mug she was drinking from down by the chair and went back to her pose.

I would have gladly given Jerica the mug Valena handed me.

That was possibly the strongest, worst tasting coffee I had ever experienced. My first thought was that it must have been scorched or

something. And he added sugar? Without asking? I tried to hide my reaction and set the mug on the table beside my easel.

"He likes his coffee strong," Jerica smiled. "I do too, I guess. Or at least I've learned to. You learn to tolerate things when you're married."

# Fifteen

"You okay?" Jerica asked when we got downstairs.

Theresa came out of the kitchen. "Yeah," she said, "you don't look so good." She came closer and looked at my eyes. "Valena's doctor boyfriend is here somewhere," Theresa said. "Do you want him to look at you?"

"No," I said. "It's just a headache. Probably paint fumes." That happens with oil painting sometimes. You can get sick from the fumes from the paint thinner and other solvents. Some artists wear a mask when they're using oils, which is what I should have done. I misjudged the ventilation in the room, even after I realized I couldn't open the windows. I left the door open and turned on a fan to air things out before we went to downstairs for lunch. But my headache was coming on quick. I got tired walking down the stairs behind Jerica. I decided to skip lunch with the Menkens and go home.

Amara wasn't home when I got there. She must have been having lunch with Paul or somewhere on Pearl Street. I must have fallen asleep on the couch because I don't remember her coming in. I only know that I woke up and she was there, looking down at me. I tried to stand up but fell back to the couch.

"When did you start day drinking?" Amara laughed. "That must have been some morning at the Menkens."

"I didn't." I staggered to the bathroom and threw up. I must not have looked very good when I came out and made my way back to the couch.

"And you weren't drinking?" Amara asked.

"I would think I would remember if I drank this much," I said.

Amara looked worried. "I'm not sure you'd remember anything if you drank this much," she smiled. Then she called Noah and asked it he could take me to the hospital. "But if you weren't drinking, then something is really wrong here."

The next thing I remember is waking up in a hospital bed and hearing Amara tell Noah to let the nurses know I was awake. My head was still throbbing, but I felt slightly more coherent than before.

"What happened?" I asked through the fog. "And why is this tube up my nose?"

Amara stroked my hair. "You were having some problems so we brought you to the hospital. They took some blood to run some tests then they hooked you up to all of this."

Noah came back with a doctor who seemed vaguely familiar.

"Hello, Gabriella. I'm Dr. Hickner. Let me have a look at you." He shined a light in my eyes and down my throat. "I keep thinking I know you," Dr. Hickner said as he examined me. His mouth slowly formed a slight smile. "Are you the artist that's painting that picture for the Menken family?"

"She is," Amara answered for me. "We were there the night Mrs. Menken died. That's where you saw her."

"Were you here when I came in?" I asked the doctor.

"No. I was not working last night. I didn't know you were here until I came in this morning."

"He's kind of hot," I said to Amara in drunken confidence. She flashed a grin and seemed to agree.

Dr. Hickner smiled. "That's the, uh, medication talking." He turned to Amara and Noah as he put his flashlight in his coat pocket. "Could you two please step outside for a moment?"

"Here's what we know," he said once they had left and the door was closed. "Your friends brought you here. The admitting doctor ordered a bunch of tests and found ethylene glycol in your blood stream. That's the chemical in antifreeze. You've been unconscious until now." Dr. Hickner leaned with his arms across his thighs and his interlocked fingers between his knees. "Ms. Alegré, are you doing okay? Is everything alright?"

"I'm in the hospital," I mumbled. "So things must not be alright."

"Fair point." Dr. Hickner sat upright. "I mean in your life. Have you been feeling down or depressed? Have you been sleeping a lot more or a lot less? Any stress or pressure going on?"

"A little stress," I thought I smiled but I could not feel my face so it's hard to know. "I thought antifreeze had something in it to make
it taste bad," I said.

"Antifreeze does," said Dr. Hickner. "But you can buy pure, lab grade ethylene glycol that has no taste at all. It's used in a lot of things," the doctor patiently explained. "It's also one of the solvents used in oil painting. Were you using Alkyd paints? It could have come from there. It wouldn't take much. Three ounces of that stuff, half a martini glass, is enough to kill you. And it builds up over time, or at least the effects of it do. You may have been exposed to a very small amount, but it was enough that you needed to go to the hospital."

"When we see this," the doctor continued, "it's usually because someone was trying to commit suicide. Very few people drink ethylene glycol by accident."

"Not suicide." I reached up to pull the tube from my nose but Dr. Hickner stopped me.

"Even so, when you're feeling better, I want you to talk to someone." I tried to sit up in the bed but the doctor gently pushed me back to lie down. "It's standard procedure when we see an ethylene glycol poisoning. With any luck, you'll be out of here in the morning."

I rubbed my nose and the tube that was in it. "What's this?"

"Well," said the doctor. "It should be fomepizole. That's the antidote for ethylene glycol. And it should be going into a vein in your arm, not through a tube in your nose. But we were out of fomepizole, so the doctor that saw you last night had to improvise." He checked my nose tube to make sure I hadn't moved it. "You are currently enjoying Jack Daniel's Tennessee Whiskey through your nose tube. I would let you drink it but you've been asleep until now."

"You're putting whiskey up my nose?"

"Yes. One half a gram of ethanol via commercial whiskey per kilogram of body weight at the rate of 150 milliliters per hour. But remember," he pointed his finger and mock scolded me. "We are trained professionals. Don't try this at home." Dr. Hickner sat on down in the chair beside the bed. "Sorry. Bad joke. Is there something going on that would make you want to drink antifreeze?"

It was hard to talk through the fog in my head – not to mention the throbbing in my skull – but I did my best. "No," I said. "I don't even know where I would get it. We don't have a car."

A nurse stuck her head through the door. "Her friends want to know if they can come back in now."

The doctor looked at me. "Do you feel like having visitors?"

I was already waving my hand for them to come in. "They're putting whiskey up my nose. Can you believe that?" I laughed in my drunken groggy laughing voice. "And why are you wearing a wedding gown? Are you two getting married?"

"I'm a statue on Pearl Street," Amara explained to the doctor. "We were in such a rush to get here that I didn't take time to change clothes." She smiled and straightened up my hair. "I've been here all night. I guess I should have gone home to change."

"Your friends saved your life by bringing you in early," Dr. Hickner explained. He turned to Amara and Paul. "You did the right thing. Another few hours and she would have died."

Between the alcohol in the antifreeze and the whiskey they were putting up my nose, I was in no shape to have a conversation. I remember highlights but that's about it. I took Amara's hand.

"Thank you," I said. She squeezed my hand as she held it. Noah took my other hand. "Remind me later to ask you about all this," I said. "I'm probably not going to remember much of this when I get home."

Amara wiped a tear from her cheek. "I promise."

"You kissed Valena!" I said way too loudly and with way too much laughter. "We saw you!"

"That's the alcohol talking," Amara said.

"He's kind of hot, don't you think?" I said to Amara. "Oh, Noah. I'm sorry." I took Noah's hand. "You're way hotter than he is, even if he is a doctor."

The handsome young doctor's face turned red as he struggled to regain his professional composure. He turned away from me to talk to Amara and Noah. "She should be fine by tomorrow."

"I'm painting the Menken family," I blurted out. My words slurred together. "It's going to be a really, really big painting." I held out my hands out to demonstrate the dimensions of seven feet wide and four feet tall canvas.

"Yes you are," the doctor laughed. He turned back to Amara and Noah. "You saved her life. Another twelve hours and she would have been dead. I'm going to keep her here overnight for observation."

"What he means," I whispered loudly to Amara, "is that he wants to make sure I'm not suicidal."

"There is that, yes," Dr. Hickner said. "It's also a hospital protocol. When someone ingests ethylene glycol, we like to keep them around and see how they're doing. But also because I want to make sure there's no kidney damage or other complications."

"He's a good doctor," I told Amara. Then I snickered and covered my mouth with my hand.

"He was kissing Valena."

# Sixteen

I called Theresa the next morning after I'd been released from the hospital and my head no longer felt like an enraged timpani player was trapped inside my skull. For what it's worth, I do not recommend consuming Tennessee whiskey through a nasogastric tube.

I was surprised to hear Carson's voice on the phone. "Hey Gabriella. Theresa is in the shower but I saw it was you so I picked it up. Still have a headache?"

"No. I'm not sure what brought that on," I lied. I also wasn't sure how Carson knew I had a headache. Jerica must have told him. Hopefully the doctor hadn't told Valena I was in the hospital.

"Just one of those things," I said. "Paint fumes, maybe? I'll be sure and turn on a fan when I go back up there." I really did not want to talk to Carson so I rushed into what I had to say. "I need to do some things this morning. Could you tell Theresa that I'll be in to paint this afternoon and that she only needs to call me if that doesn't work for her. Otherwise, I'll just see her after lunch, say, around one."

"Around one," he repeated. "Got it."

"And then after her, I'll get to Valena." I tried to sound excited before I ended the call. It occurred to me that Carson might not be the best person to trust with a message if he was, in fact, the person who tried to kill me. Or Jerica. If he had ever killed anyone, for that matter. I sent a text to Theresa telling her I would be in around one just in case.

My next call was to Officer Singer at the Boulder Police Department.

"Someone at the Menken house tried to kill me yesterday. They tried to poison me," I told the officer. "And I think they did the same thing to Mrs. Menken. I think that's how she died, from gradual poisoning with ethylene glycol."

"Whoa. Wait a minute." I could hear one of Boulder's Finest chewing over the phone, followed by the gurgling sound of what must have been him drinking through a straw from an empty cup.

"Okay," he said. "How do you know they tried to poison you?"

"Because I just got out of the hospital after being treated for ethylene glycol poisoning," I told him. "That's the chemical in antifreeze."

"I know what it is," he said. "Why would someone want to poison you?"

"I don't know. Maybe they think I might figure out who killed Mrs. Menken."

"And you don't think Mrs. Menken died of natural causes even though the doctor" – he said this next part really slowly – "*her own personal doctor* filled out the death certificate. I know you like to pretend to be a detective. Are you pretending to be a doctor now, too?"

"I'm not pretending anything," I protested. "I ended up in the hospital and they had to treat me for ethylene glycol poisoning." I left out the part about funneling whiskey up my nose with a tube. I'd already heard enough jokes about that from Noah and Amara.

"Okay. Let's say you're right. Do you know who did this?"

"I have a good idea," I said.

"I can't arrest someone based on a 'good idea', Gabriella," the officer reminded me. "I'm going to need something more than that. Bring me some evidence and we'll talk. Until then, I have to go with the official cause of death for Mrs. Menken."

"What about me?" I protested. "Do I have to die before you will investigate who tried to kill me?"

To his credit, Officer Singer managed to sound less condescending after my outburst. "No. And I am sorry this happened to you. But you have to give me something to work with. Right now, all I have is your 'good idea.' That's not enough to make an arrest."

"And you can't go over there and look around?" I asked.

"I can't even get a search warrant with what you've told me here," he said. "Sorry."

Amara was at the kitchen table, scrolling her phone in search of something we could afford. Our pending eviction, through no fault of our own, was creating a major inconvenience in our lives, especially for Amara. I'd been so busy with the portrait that I had turned all of that over to her. She didn't seem to mind, but I still felt guilty about it. I'd also been neglecting my early morning art therapy sessions. I hadn't seen the sunrise since I started working on the portrait.

"This thing is consuming my life," I said.

"You mean the portrait?" Amara asked. "Sounds like it almost ended your life, if what you said yesterday is true. Of course, you were pretty out of it. Not sure you'd want to remember most of what you said."

I felt my face heat up as I blushed. "Great. Anything really embarrassing?"

"I'm sure Noah felt flattered, once you convinced him that you'd rather sleep with him than with the doctor."

"Seriously? I said that?"

"All that and more, as they say." Amara was enjoying this way too much. "Remind me to get you wasted more often."

I wondered how much damage control I was going to have to do. Hopefully Noah wouldn't hold what I said while in my drunken altered state against me.

"What do you remember about yesterday?" Amara asked. "And how did you manage to swallow antifreeze?"

"I remember drinking the worst coffee I'd ever had," I said. "Valena brought it up."

"Do you think Valena was trying to kill you?"

"I don't know." I gathered my thoughts as my memory came into focus. "And I remember her giving me a specific coffee mug, like that was the mug she wanted me to have."

"What was so special about that mug?" Amara asked.

The memories of yesterday were becoming clearer. "I think it was Jerica's mug? Maybe. I don't know." I thought some more. "The mug belonged to Mrs. Menken, but Jerica apparently had been using it since she got here." I sat up as my head rose above the fog. "Jerica had given the mug to her mother. That's why she kept using it."

"But Valena gave it to you instead of Jerica? That's a jerk thing to do." Amara's eyes grew wider. "Do you think Valena meant to kill

Jerica? Was that why she put her coffee in that mug?"

"But if she was trying to poison Jerica, why would she give the mug to me? That doesn't make any sense. No. Valena knew what she was doing with the mugs. She was looking at Jerica when she handed it to me."

"Maybe she changed her mind at the last minute," Amara said. "This is her sister we're talking about."

"Yeah, but I bet the same thing happened to Mrs. Menken," I said. "If someone is willing to kill their mother, they're probably okay with killing their sister."

"Who else could have put something in that mug?" Amara reached for the black jellybeans that she eats when she's in deep thought.

I remembered Valena saying that Carson and Theresa were in the kitchen.

"Carson!" My loud response made my own head hurt. "Carson made the coffee. I remember Jerica talking about how he made it really strong. It really was horrible tasting coffee."

"I don't think anything would taste very good with antifreeze in it," Amara offered. "That's not really a fair judgement on the quality of the barista or the coffee."

I took the jellybean jar from Amara. It was my turn for deep thoughts. "Is it possible," I said while chewing, "that Carson was trying to kill Jerica?" I stood up and started pacing in front of our couch. "What if he used that mug because he knew Jerica would take it but then Valena gave it to me out of spite?"

"That makes sense," Amara said. "In some strange, twisted sibling rivalry, obnoxious little sister kind of way, as long as Valena wasn't there when he added in his secret ingredient. Was anyone else in the house?"

"Let me think." I went over the day as best I could. "I saw Theresa and Destiny. The only one who wasn't in the house was Alyssa."

"That's not helpful," Amara said. "I mean, I guess it rules out Alyssa and Oswald as suspects, but it still could have been any of the four people that were in the house."

"Don't be so sure about Alyssa or Oswald. Just because I didn't see them doesn't mean they weren't there or weren't involved." I remembered how Alyssa walked right through the front door without so much as a knock or a hello on the morning I did her part of the portrait.

Amara was thinking more quickly than I was. "Didn't you say that Theresa was in the kitchen with Carson?"

"Yeah, but why would Theresa want to poison her sister?" I picked up Miss Marple and put her on my lap. "Whoever it was, I think we can rule out natural causes for Mrs. Menken," I said. "I looked up the symptoms of ethylene glycol poisoning. It's not good." The list ended with coma and death. I was lucky that Amara found me and got me to the hospital in time.

"Thank you," I said as I hugged Amara. I felt a wave of emotion that I chose to believe was the residual influence of alcohol ingestion.

"For what?" she asked.

"For being there," I said. "Thank you." I took a moment to reset. "Mrs. Menken was showing signs of antifreeze poisoning when she talked to me that morning. I just didn't know it because, seriously, who thinks of these things? The tremors, her speech, how unsteady she was on her feet. All of that was right there. I thought it was because she was old."

Amara was still skeptical. "So why did you end up in the hospital and she didn't?"

"I ended up in the hospital because you took me there. Otherwise, I would have slept on the couch until I sobered up enough to walk and would eventually have had kidney failure and the rest of it, maybe even the aforementioned coma and death."

"I really never woke you up," Amara said. "I called Noah and he helped me pour you into his car."

"But what if there was no one to take Mrs. Menken to the hospital?" I asked. "No one to wake her up or who would even check on her?" *Or*, I thought, *no one who would take her to a doctor even if they*
*knew she was dying?*

I tried to compare what happened to me with what little I knew about Mrs. Menken. "One sip of coffee was enough for me to know I didn't want any more, but I don't know how much antifreeze was in that sip. It takes about three ounces of antifreeze to kill you in one dose. I can't imagine drinking three ounces of that." I went to the cabinet and got a glass. "This holds eight ounces. Imagine this glass almost half full of antifreeze." I turned on the faucet and filled the glass to just below half. "That's enough to kill you."

I emptied the glass and put it back in the cabinet. "But what if she was getting it a little at a time over several days? A tiny amount at a time wouldn't be as noticeable." I turned to face Amara. "You might not even taste it, depending on what it was mixed with. And the doctor even said that lab-grade ethylene had no taste or smell. You could drink that and not know it."

I tried to remember what else the doctor said and what I had read online. "This stuff doesn't really leave your system unless you do something to get it out. Regular alcohol doesn't stay in the body very long, really. But ethylene glycol isn't like regular alcohol. The residue builds up in the body over time, mainly in the kidneys. A little bit at a time, in juice, coffee, or in Mrs. Menken's evening martini, over several days would have the same lethal effect. At first she might look like she was drunk or just a little buzzed, like she did that morning I saw her. Eventually, she would get a rapid pulse, congestive heart failure, fluid in the lungs, kidney failure, all kinds of good things. Any of which could have killed her."

"And it would look like natural causes," Amara said.

"Exactly. You're not going to find it unless you're looking for it," I said. "Which is what they did when I went to the emergency room. The doctor thought I was an attempted suicide so he had them test my blood for everything. That's how they found the ethylene glycol." I sat back down on the couch. "They would have found it in Mrs. Menken if they had done an autopsy. But nobody wanted to do that."

"Valena wanted an autopsy," Amara reminded me.

"Right," I said. "And then she kissed the man who officially decided there would not be one."

# Seventeen

For someone who couldn't wait to get started, Theresa was strangely absent when I arrived at the Menken house after lunch. Destiny greeted me at the door. She put down her camera long enough to tell me Theresa wasn't there.

"Do you record everything all the time?" I asked.

"Yeah," the Dark One said from behind the camera.

"I've been thinking about our conversation," I said.

Destiny's face twisted up into a puzzled look. "About removing the rough spots?"

I realized that she might not want to talk about the murder in the house where it took place, especially if the killer was here right now. "Yeah," I said softly. "That. Do you think you've recorded anything that could help?"

Destiny put the camera down. "Not sure. I'll have to look."

Valena came out of the kitchen with a coffee mug just as I was going up the stairs. "If you're looking for Theresa," she called out, "she's not back yet."

"Think anyone would care if I went on up?" I asked.

"I don't care," Valena said. "Go do what you need to do."

I could hear Carson and Jerica arguing in the kitchen as I walked to the stairs. Jerica wanted Carson to get back to the ranch to take care of things. Carson didn't seem to want to go. I've never been married, but it sounded like the kind of argument that might happen when marriage partners are also business partners. I kept my head down and hoped they didn't notice me.

The argument grew fainter as I walked up the stairs. I knew there were people in the house, but the open bedroom door at the top of the stairway was too tempting to pass up. I peeked inside.

Jerica's baseball cap was on the bed among the throw pillows on the unmade bed. A belt with Carson's oversized cowboy belt buckle was draped over the back of a chair. I didn't see anything that might have been helpful to my investigation about Mrs. Menken or me. I also did not want to get caught rummaging through their stuff. I'd been in the house too many times to claim that I was lost. I moved on to the next room to see what was there.

Even though Destiny and Valena were officially only visiting their mother's house and did not live there, at least not most of the time, their unique individual style was as present in their bedrooms as it was in the clothes they wore. I ignored what was obviously Destiny's room with its big computer monitors and dark atmosphere and headed towards Valena's room.

As fit her personality, Valena's room used a much brighter color palette. Its southern exposure meant more light than Destiny's northern facing room. So did the white walls and white rug that covered the space beneath and around the bed. The bed was covered in a thick, slightly peach colored comforter with matching pillow cases. A white table sat below a mirror framed in round lights. A white director's chair with "VALENA" stenciled on the back was the room's only personalization. I looked at the assortment of makeup brushes and wondered which medium – oils, acrylics, watercolors – would work best with each, or if they would even work for paints at all.

Valena's room also had all the signs of a boyfriend who spent a lot of time there. A pair of men's shoes were beside the bed. A man's shirt and a necktie were draped across the back of a chair. I recognized Dr. Hickner's sunglasses on a nightstand beside the bed, along with an almost depleted prescription pad. The closet door was open so I peeked in. Sitting on top of some shelves were two canvas wig stands. One wig was red. The other was the same color as Destiny's preferred hair coloring.

I carefully closed Valena's door and went on down the hallway. The clothes on the bed and the décor of the next room all pointed to Theresa. My host had created a cozy sanctuary of lavender and off-white, with wide open windows and plenty of very healthy plants.

There, in plain sight on a nightstand beside the bed, beneath a tawdry romance novel that was open with the text side down – what
kind of heathen leaves a book that way? – was the last Will and Testament of Mrs. Avyanna Menken.

"This must have been what she was looking at in her mother's bedroom that day," I said to no one.

I carefully slid the single page document out from under the book for a closer look. It was surprisingly brief, especially for someone whose estate was as complicated as the Menken empire.

"I, Avyanna Menken, being of sound mind and body, do hereby give my home and all my possessions to my beloved daughter, Theresa Menken. Furthermore, I give Theresa Menken full control of my estate to dispose of as she sees fit. For reasons known to each of them, my other daughters Alyssa, Jerica, Valena, and Destiny are to receive a total of one dollar which they may divide among themselves as they wish."

The document was signed and dated on the day of Mrs. Menken's death. To be clear, the name had been printed below her signature in very clear, very steady handwriting.

The voices from downstairs were getting louder. Jerica and Carson must have moved their argument from the kitchen to someplace near the foot of the stairs. I put the unfolded Will on the bed and took a picture of it. Then I carefully returned it to its place beneath the book.

I hurried down the hall to set up my paints. I tried to look like I'd been waiting there for some time when Theresa walked in.
"Sorry I'm late," Theresa said when she walked in a few minutes behind me. "Let me go change. I'll only be a second."

I spent the next ten minutes hoping I hadn't moved anything and praying that Theresa wasn't very attentive in case I had.

"I think this is the right look," Theresa said when she returned. "Same outfit." She glanced at the mirror. "The hair and the makeup are close enough." She looked at the photograph for her pose and did her best to recreate it.

"You look fine," I told her. "Remember, we're not doing that much detail today. Just the first coat."

"Mother looks happy in that picture," she said. "I'm glad she was having a good day. That wasn't always the case, but she was having a good day that day. It got that way towards the end, you know. She had good days and bad days. She was beginning to slip a little, mentally, I mean. Wasn't quite as sharp as she was before. The two of us did our best to keep up appearances, to hide the fact that she was becoming more forgetful. We stopped going out as much, stopped talking to friends. And she was getting shaky, physically, I mean. I'm not even sure that Alyssa or any of the others noticed it, although they would have if they'd spent enough time with her. If they did, none of them said anything. They weren't as close to her as I was."

Thresa looked at her mother in the picture once more. "She wanted people to remember her being as smart and strong willed as she ever was, not as some frail, forgetful old lady who couldn't take care of herself. I wanted that for her."

My mind went back to when I met Mrs. Menken that morning at my cart. She was coherent and clear. She was not some lost person wandering the streets. We didn't talk long, but she seemed like she was in full control of everything she was saying at the time. She was a bit shaky, but I would not describe her as "frail." The only indication that anything was wrong was her slightly slurred speech and the tremors in her hands, symptoms that I later knew could be attributed to antifreeze poisoning. She was certainly in command of her faculties when she was negotiating the price of the portrait.

Theresa stepped into position. "I did that for the past two years, taking time off work and giving up my social life so I could help her keep her secret and her dignity. That's why I moved in. Alyssa didn't even know I was living here until a couple of months ago, which tells you how often Alyssa visited her mother, and the others didn't care. It was easier for me to move in so I could help out, maybe keep an eye on her at night in case there was a problem. I guess that makes me 'the good daughter,' right?"

"You wanted to help her keep her dignity," I said. "That's a very loving thing to do, especially for someone like your mother. I'm sure she appreciated that. I would."

"Exactly," Theresa said. "People deserve to be remembered at their best. Healthy in mind and body and with all their mental faculties in place. That became even more important to me towards the end, when she started to decline more quickly."

"And yet," I said, "she was healthy enough to hike Trail Ridge with you the week before she died. Wasn't that what you were telling me?"

"Where she lost another water bottle," Theresa chuckled. "She wanted to do that. She loved the mountains. Like I said, she had good days and bad days. That day on Trail Ridge was a very good day. And she was having a very good day, relatively speaking, on the day she died. She was excited about this portrait. This was important to her. That's why I thought we should go ahead and do it as if she was still here. It's like fulfilling her last wish."

Theresa's comment about the water bottle reminded me that I still had Mrs. Menken's bottle at my house from when she left it at my cart. I tried to remember where. I stopped talking as I worked on the contours of her face. I didn't say anything until I was blocking out her shoulders.

"What you're saying sounds like a lot of work and stress on you," I said. "Were the others any help with her at all?"

"Are you kidding? Alyssa is too busy with her job. Jerica only visits once or twice a year. She wasn't even aware of the problem. Valena and Destiny are too self-absorbed to notice much of anything that isn't in a mirror or a video. No. It was her secret and I was glad to help her keep it."

Destiny came through the door with her camera, but Theresa had nothing left to say. Either that, or she didn't want to put her comments on record. Destiny was in the room for about fifteen minutes before she left as silently as she had come in.

"Want to take a break?" I asked my model. "Fifteen minutes is a long time to stand in one position."

"No, I'm fine. But I could use something to drink." I assumed she was going to the kitchen when she left the room. Then I heard her voice from the other end of the hallway, near the spiral staircase.

"Valena? Valena. Be a dear and bring me a glass of wine from that bottle in the fridge." She came back to the studio but just stuck her head in the door.

"Want Valena to bring you anything?"

"No," I smiled as best I could. "I'm good."

Theresa stepped into position and back into her pose. Valena smiled at me as she carried the wineglass to Theresa.

"When is it my turn?" Valena asked. I didn't look at her. I couldn't. But I did manage to say what needed to be said.

"Right after Destiny."

It was late in the afternoon when I finished painting Theresa. Destiny must have passed her on the stairs. She was in my studio before I had time to clean my palette.

"Valena said I was next? Is that right?" She pointed to the clock. "Do we still have time?"

I didn't have the time but I wanted to talk to Destiny and painting her was the easiest way to do that. "Sure," I said. "Stand right there and let's get started."

Destiny was wearing the same outfit that she wore in the photograph. No piercings and no hat. Her hair and makeup were exactly as they were in the photograph.

Destiny and Valena were sitting on the floor in the photo. They would be at the bottom edge of the canvas. I needed to raise the easels so I could reach it. "We're going to need some help moving this," I explained to Destiny. "Is Valena down there?"

Destiny went downstairs and returned with her sister. For the first time, I was looking at the twins side by side. "I could almost do this part with either one of you," I joked. "Just change the hair color and makeup. Two for one." The clones who worked so hard to be unique were not amused. It took some doing, but the three of us were able to raise the canvas to a workable height. I still needed to figure out a way for Destiny to recreate how she was sitting in the photograph on a stool or something, but at least I could get her face. I could do the rest from the photograph.

"Want me to get your camera and record this for you?" Valena asked her sister.

Destiny did not like that idea. "Please don't. And please don't hang around while we're doing this."

"Whatever you want." Valena looked at me. "Are you sure you don't want anything to drink before I am banished from the room? Coffee? Wine?"

I felt an involuntary shudder go down my spine. "No thank you. I'm avoiding alcohol for the time being."

"Suit yourself," she smiled. "I thought I'd ask before I left."

My model seemed to relax a bit once her sister left.

"Have you had a chance to go through your videos?" I asked as I painted the contours of her face.

"I did," she said. "Come with me." I followed Destiny into the bathroom I used to wash my brushes. She locked the door and handed one earbud to me. The other she put in her ear. Then she handed me her phone and hit "play." I put the small screen at an angle that both of us could see.

"This is just a clip," Destiny said. "I have a longer segment on my computer. I cut this out to show you, but you can watch the longer video if you want."

The clip began with Valena coming into the kitchen.

"Where were you when you recorded this?" I asked while we watched Valena open a cabinet to get a glass.

"At the kitchen table," Destiny said. "I recorded it on my phone. Either they didn't notice or they're just so used to me recording things that they forgot I was there."

On the video, Valena leaned up against the counter. "Kurt told me that Gabriella went to the emergency room last night. Antifreeze poisoning. She almost died. You won't believe how they brought her back."

Theresa ignored the last part of what Valena said and focused on the doctor's conduct instead. "I thought doctors weren't supposed to talk about their patients," Theresa said. "Isn't that a HIPPA violation or something?"

Valena put her glass on the marble countertop then hopped up to sit beside it. "You'd be amazed at what doctors are not supposed to talk about," she said. "Has Gabriella said anything to either of you about going to the hospital?"

"No," said Carson. "But you've got to wonder why someone would try to commit suicide like that. Did she change her mind after she drank it or someone find her and bring her in?"

Valena almost answered but she was interrupted by Theresa. "Would a suicidal person like that try to harm other people?"

The video shook on the screen. "Sorry," Destiny said. "That was me moving around. I almost dropped the camera." On the video, Teresa looked at Carson. "Should we do something before she tries to take one of us out with her? Should we tell her not to come back?"

The doorbell rang before Valena or Carson could answer Theresa's question. "That's her," Valena said. "What should I tell her?"

Carson looked at Theresa and then at Valena. "Nothing," he said. "If she wants you to know, she'll tell you. Just watch out." The video ended with Valena leaving the kitchen.

Destiny looked at me when the video finished. "That's all I got. I went out the back door in the kitchen before they saw me."
"Isn't that the door that goes to the garage?" I asked.

"It is," Destiny said. "And before you ask, I already checked. There's a container of lab-grade ethylene glycol on a shelf by the door. Hiding in plain sight. All we had to do was know what we were looking for."

"They're going to be looking for us if we stay in here much longer," I said. "We should get to work. We left the bathroom and got to work on the portrait. Neither one of us had much to say. I was able to paint much faster when I wasn't trying to carry on a conversation.

"There," I said. "Finished, at least for now."

Destiny looked at her portion of the portrait. "That looks good," she said. "You should leave it like this, with only one color." She slowly walked the length of the canvas, studying the details or the lack there of in each face. "Isn't da Vinci's *La Scapigliata* considered to
be unfinished?"

"You mean his picture of the lady with disheveled hair?" That's the literal translation of *La Scapigliata,* "Lady with Disheveled Hair." I made a mental note to whisper that to Noah some time. "That's a beautiful picture I said. And it is all in that same umber color." I touched up a spot on the canvas.

"But why would I do that with such a colorful family?"

# Eighteen

It was almost eight-thirty when I left the Menken's house. I told the Uber driver to take me to our house. Amara wasn't there. I sent her a text. On a hunch, I grabbed Mrs. Menken's water bottle. There was still some liquid in it. I put the water bottle in the freezer to test my hypothesis.

Amara still had not responded to my text about dinner. Either she was still working and couldn't read her phone or she was spending time with Paul and did not want to be interrupted. I walked over to Pearl Street to see if she was there.

John Spool was sitting on a bench near his spot. His guitar was already in its case and on the ground beside him like a loyal service animal. He motioned me over when he saw me.

"Taking off early?" I asked.

"Taking off period," he said. "Someone stole my tip jar. It was probably only a hundred dollars or so, but still. I think it was a sign."

I don't usually put the word 'only' in the same sentence as "a hundred dollars." That's three caricatures for me. I'm not sure how many hours of playing songs it took John to make that.

"That's horrible. Any idea who?"

"No. I broke a string and turned around to get another one out of my case. I had to do some digging to find the right one. That's when they grabbed it."

I knew better than to try and guess who would do such a thing. Pearl Street is a mixture of artists, academics, hippies, hipsters, and homeless. And tourists. It could be anyone.

"It was a sign," John repeated. "It's time for me to go back to where I came from. Back to Memphis."

"You shouldn't have any trouble selling your place," I said. Since we got that letter, Amara and I had been watching the real estate sites close enough to know that properties didn't stay on the market very long. And the closer the property was to Pearl Street, the faster it seemed to sell.

"Your place will sell as soon as you list it." I raised a single finger. "One week, tops." I didn't want to think about what a two-story, business/apartment combo on Pearl Street might be worth. "Or I guess you could rent it."

"Don't want to rent," he said. "Don't want to deal with it." He turned to me. "I'm hungry. Want to go to Papa's?"

"Only if you let me pay for it." I knew John had money even after having his day's earnings stolen, but I felt bad that some loser would steal from a busker. What kind of person does that?

He smiled. "Sure, now that you're a big-time portrait artist. Let's go eat."

We were walking up the street to Papa's when I heard Amara call my name. John and I stopped to wait for her to catch up. She was in her *Cowgirl* outfit.

"We're going to grab something to eat," I told her. "Want to join us?"

John smiled at Amara. "Please do," he said. Then he turned to me. "Want to get Noah?"

I had to laugh. "Noah is in bed by now, or he's about to be. Three in the morning comes really early."

We had just placed our orders when John asked me why I became an artist.

"I don't know." I swirled the ice around in my drink. "I just always did it."

"Right. Same with my guitar. But how did you know that you wanted to spend your life doing it? When did you get serious about it?"

That took some thought. "Well," I said as felt the cold condensation on my glass, "I wasn't planning on being a caricature artist on a street somewhere, if that's what you're asking. I kind of fell into this."

"But you didn't fall into art," Amara said. "At some point, you had to decide that you weren't going to work in a bank or whatever and that you were going to do this. Those were my choices. I chose to do what I do because I like doing it."

"I became an artist because I couldn't not become one," I said. "I was going to be an artist regardless. I just had to find a way to get paid to do it. And I did. Sort of. On good days."

"So you're going to stay here a while?" John asked.

"I hope to move on, eventually. Career wise, I mean. Not be a busker. I need a more steady income, or at least make enough that I can survive when business is slow. I would love to have a studio here on Pearl Street, somewhere where I could display something the size of the Menken portrait along with other pieces. I'm glad Noah has my stuff in his shop, but I would love to have somewhere where I could have a gallery and a studio all in the same building. Maybe do some classes. Those paint and sip places are really popular right now."

"Pearl Street would be a good location for something like that," John said.

"It would be if I could afford it," I said.

"Prices are high right now," he said, "but I don't want to sell my building." He looked into his glass. "And I absolutely do not want to rent it. Hempy was a good tenant, but I've heard too many horror stories about people tearing things up or being late with payments. I don't want to have to deal with that, especially if I'm not living here."

He smiled at me and Amara. "I need a house sitter."

"You can find those online," I said. "Someone would love to house sit in a place like yours." I thought about it for a moment. "This is temporary? You're planning on coming back? Is that why you don't want to sell?"

"I do not want to sell." John leaned across the table and smiled even more. "And I am not planning on coming back."

He looked in my eyes and spoke very slowly. "And I would like to find a house sitter."

Amara punched my arm. "I thought you were a sleuth! How are you not getting this?" she said. She looked at John. "YES! We would be glad to house sit for you for as long as you need."

"Thank you," John said. "I was beginning to think I was going to have to draw a picture for the artist here." He held up his water glass for a toast.

"Here's to making changes," said our new patron. Our three glasses clinked together.

I felt my face turning red. And my smile spreading across my face. And, if I'm honest, a few tears in my eyes.

"To making changes."

***

I woke up the next morning wondering if the previous night's conversation with John was a dream or if I still had some residual ethylene glycol or whiskey somewhere in my system. I also thought about the implications if John was serious. It meant that we wouldn't have to leave Pearl Street. Far from leaving it, we would be closer than I ever imagined. With a gallery and the space to set up a real studio. Amara could even use part of it as a dance studio if she wanted.

I did not expect and would never ask to be paid for figuring out who killed Pello and keeping John out of prison for a murder he did not commit. We really never talked about it. He came by and said thank you. That was enough. Was this his way of paying me back? I hope he didn't feel like he had to do that, but I was glad that Amara and I no longer had to worry about where we were going to live.

It also meant I could return Mrs. Menken's check and leave before someone poisoned me again. I knew I might not be so lucky next time. I tried to think of why someone might want to kill me, assuming it was me they were trying to kill and not Jerica.

I was trying not to think about the fact that someone tried to kill me with antifreeze. But that thought kept getting stronger as my thinking grew clearer. Knowing that it might have been an accident and that the poison was meant for another person did not make it any better.

"Jerica," I thought. "I need to warn Jerica."

I just didn't know who to warn Jerica to watch out for. It had to be someone who knew about the investigation. Alyssa knew, but she didn't seem like the type of person who would tell the rest of the family. "Although," I said to no one. "I could picture Alyssa telling Theresa."

Destiny sounded like she had figured it out when I saw her on Pearl Street but then she acted like she had no idea when I asked her about it at her sitting. I was still trying to figure out what could cause that kind of almost dissociative split. For all her goth darkness, Destiny seemed very fragile. Maybe disassociation was her way of coping with everything that had happened.

I had some theories but no clear idea of who might want me to stop the investigation. Carson, Valena, and Theresa seemed like the most likely suspects, but it was circumstantial at best. I had no proof of anything. Certainly not enough evidence to go to the police. I still wasn't sure about Dr. Kurt Hickner. I had thought he saved my life until Amara told me that he wasn't the doctor on duty the night they took me to the emergency room. He didn't come in until the next morning. By that time, I was already on my way to getting better. Still, he could have killed me then if he wanted to but he didn't.

And then there was dear Mrs. Menken herself. Between the portrait at the Menken house and the dozens of practice sketches and paintings I had done at home, I'd spent no telling how many hours looking at her face. She trusted me to do a portrait of her family, people she loved, even if she had some bizarre ways of showing it. I felt like I owed it to her to finish what I had started, not only with the painting but with the investigation as well.

Avyanna Menken deserved justice. Her daughters, at least the ones that didn't kill her, deserved to know what happened to their mother. I deserved to know who tried to kill me. I owed all of us that much.

I opened the freezer to see what my options were for dinner and saw Mrs. Menken's water bottle. Whatever was in it was still liquid. The water bottle was in the freezer for almost twenty-four hours and the liquid inside it did not freeze.

By definition, that made it antifreeze.

Amara emerged from her bedroom to find me swirling the liquid in the water bottle and staring into the open top.

"That's the trouble with those things," she said. "You have to watch them all the time."

"This is antifreeze," I told her. "And this is Mrs. Menken's water bottle, the water bottle that she had that morning and left at my cart." I swirled the liquid around inside the water bottle. "Someone put antifreeze in Mrs. Menken's water bottle."

"Didn't we kind of already know that?" Amara said.

"We suspected it, especially after what happened to me. But without an autopsy, this is the closest we can get to proving the connection."

# Nineteen

Valena met me at the front door the next morning wearing the same clothes she wore in the family photo. Her hair and makeup were perfect.

"You're the last one for this part," I said. "Thanks for being so patient."

I'd learned some conversational skills during my time on Pearl Street. I'm not as smooth as John Spool, but I can get almost anyone to talk to me. I've persuaded more than a few shy pedestrians who were on the bubble to go ahead and get a caricature or a portrait. "You know you want to," was my usual closer, followed with "It would look great in your office," or whatever seemed appropriate. I've never tried to make small talk with someone who had tried to murder me. What do you say in that situation?

Not that I wished that Valena had given the mug to Jerica instead of me. Far from it. I liked Jerica. I had some serious misgivings about her husband, but I wasn't going to hold that against her. We've all made mistakes. She just happened to marry hers. I wondered if he wasn't somehow involved in trying to kill me. Or Jerica.

Or, for that matter, Avyanna Menken.

"I am ready to go," I announced with my paint brush in hand. "Let's do this." I was about to cover the only remaining white space of the canvas. The rest was painted in burnt sienna pigment. It's misleading to say it was all one color. There were inflections of color, bolder strokes in some places, less bold lines or even wispy touches in others; wide strokes between the sisters and finer, more detailed work on their faces. It was all the same earth tone pigment. The difference was in the pressure and the movement of the brush.

"You're not saying much," Valena observed. "I've been in here when you were painting the others. You were more talkative with them. Except for Destiny."

I smiled but kept on painting. I had to make sure my anger and fear didn't show up in the portrait.

Angry art has its place, but I didn't think Valena would like it if she looked like she was drawn by an enraged painter or that Theresa would appreciate a violent picture hanging above her couch. Then again, I wasn't sure how Theresa might feel about having a portrait of the woman who killed her mother hanging above her couch either, even if the killer was part of the family. I wondered if there might come a time when Theresa or Alyssa would ask me to come back and cover the killer like a bad tattoo. I suppose I could put in a big tree or some shrubbery. That is, if the killer actually was one of the sisters and not Carson or someone else.

"Tell me about your handsome young doctor," I asked.

"Kurt?" Valena smiled. "Nice guy. Good friend. I honestly believe he would do anything in the world for me. He was Mother's doctor. That's how we met. He came over here to check on her and I happened to answer the door. The first time was a coincidence. I didn't know who he was." She flipped her hair away from her face. "It was no accident when I went to the door after that. We started talking. He started coming over more often. That was probably the best medical care Mother ever had." Her mouth twisted into a smirking smile. "And she never even thanked me."

"He kept her healthy," I said. I stepped back to look at my progress and then at Valena.

"He did," Valena said. "Not that it was that hard of a job. She was in good shape for someone her age. That's why we were all so surprised when she died. It just didn't seem possible."

"I thought Dr. Hickner said she had some heart problems. That's why he didn't do an autopsy, right?"

"Right," she said. "And maybe she did. I don't know. But she was always walking. She hiked. She stayed busy." Valena shifted her weight on the stool. "Theresa thought Mother was slipping – that was Theresa's word for it, 'slipping' – but I didn't see it. I think Theresa used that as an excuse to move in here and run Mother's life. A chance to be the good daughter." Valena gazed through the glass. "Apparently it worked."

"Please stay still," I reminded her. "Why do you say that?"

"No reason," Valena said. "We'll know when they read the Will."

I finished Valena's section of the portrait. The entire canvas was covered in different shades of burnt sienna. The skeleton of the painting was there. I only had to fill in the details and the colors.

Valena left as I was cleaning up. I was about to leave when Jerica walked into the studio. She stopped in front of the canvas. "That looks really good." She turned to me. "And before you say anything, yes, I know it isn't finished."

"Thanks," I said. "I thought we could paint you tomorrow so you can get out of here and get back home."

"It's no rush," she said. "I was thinking about staying until it's finished so I could be here for the big unveiling." She took a sip from the coffee mug she had in her hand. It was the same mug Valena had given to me a few days before. The mug that sent me to the hospital.

I put my hand on the mug before Jerica could drink from it. "I have to tell you something. Have a seat. May I?" I took the mug and put it on the table. Then I shut the door and sat facing Jerica.

"Please listen very carefully," I said. "Someone in this house tried to kill me. That mug," I pointed to Jerica's mug, "had antifreeze mixed with the coffee."

"How do you know that?"

"Because I ended up in the hospital with a tube up my nose. It was ethylene glycol. Antifreeze."

Jerica was understandably confused and upset. "Are you saying that someone put antifreeze in our coffee that day? I didn't get sick."

"Then it wasn't in both mugs," I said. "Because if it was, you would know. But it was in the one that Valena gave to me."

Jerica must have been thinking back to that day. "I'd been using that mug since we got here. Do you think someone meant for me to drink it and Valena mixed up the mugs? Who would want me dead?"

"Who else was in the kitchen that day?" I asked.

Jerica's eyebrows went up as her jaw went completely slack. "It was Theresa and Carson." She swallowed and raised her chin.

"And Valena," she continued. "And Destiny was probably here but she wasn't in the kitchen that morning. At least I didn't see her."

"Was Alyssa there?" I asked.

Jerica shook her head. She got up from her chair. "I don't know what to say."

"There's something else," I told her. "Your mother left her water bottle at my booth that day. There was antifreeze in there, too."

"You mean that whoever did that to you may also have killed Mother?" Jerica sat back down. She put her face in her hands. "We need to tell someone," she said.

"I told the police," I said, "but they need more evidence, especially since there was no autopsy."

Jerica kept shaking her head back and forth. Finally she looked up. "I hate to say this, but could we exhume Mother's body and see if she drank this stuff?"

"That won't work," I said. "They use those same chemicals when they embalm someone. You would expect to find ethylene glycol in an embalmed body." I sat down and took Jerica's hands. "I wish I could tell you more, but I thought you should know what I know. I'm sorry."

I finished packing up my brushes and headed for the door. Jerica stayed in the studio. I waved goodbye to Theresa as I walked out the door.

The realization that I could have died was growing stronger every day. I didn't want to think about it. I got home, took a shower, and invited my favorite distraction over for dinner.

***

"You told her?" Noah asked the next morning, as I told him what I said to Jerica and nibbled on cold leftover Pad Thai for breakfast. Noah rarely took the mornings off. I was thrilled when he finally hired someone who could open the cupcake shop. Why did I decide to ruin the morning by talking about the Menkens?

Noah repeated his question very slowly, as if English was not my native language. "You told Jerica you were poisoned?" he asked. "And then you told her it was either her sister or her husband? And that they may have intended to poison her instead?"

My breakfast nibbling turned into full blown eating. I picked out a cold piece of shrimp with my chopsticks. "I did." I put my chopsticks down. "Actually, she reached that conclusion on her own, that part about how it could have been her. But I agreed. Whoever it was could have meant that for either of us."

Noah was either overwhelmed or confused. "Why would you tell her that?"

"Because she needed to know," I said. "She deserved to know. If someone was trying to kill you, wouldn't you want to know?"

"Are you sure it was Jerica they were trying to kill?" he asked. "Sounds like they didn't want you looking around."

"It was either me or her," I said. "Maybe both of us. I don't know. Valena gave me that mug. That was very intentional. She may or may not have known what was in it. Jerica said Carson made the coffee, but Theresa was in the kitchen with him."

Amara walked into the kitchen and laughed at my breakfast. "Cold leftovers again? I can understand cold pizza, but Pad Thai? That's worse than the cold spaghetti you had the other morning," she teased. "Good morning, Noah. Didn't know you were here."

I offered to share my impromptu breakfast with Amara, but she wasn't interested. "It had to be Carson," I told Noah between bites. "No one else makes sense. Carson needed Mrs. Menken to die so he could have the money that was coming to Jerica."

Noah seemed relieved that I wasn't accusing one of his former playmates of murder. Amara wasn't convinced. She quickly pointed out what Noah and I were choosing not to see.

"You're overlooking some people," Amara said. "Valena was getting cut off. For that matter, so was Destiny. That sounds like a motive. And Theresa wanted the house. Another potentially highly motivated person who was also in the house at the time."

"But did they want those things enough to kill their own mother?" I asked.

"I don't know," Amara said. "But somebody wanted to keep a secret and they were willing to kill you to do it."

My phone rang with a call from the Boulder Police Department. "Hopefully they found a way to search that house and they found something," I said as I picked it up, although I wasn't sure what they might be looking for. Like Officer Singer said, you can find antifreeze anywhere.

"Miss Alegré? This is Officer Singer with the Boulder Police Department." He cleared his throat.

"I thought you'd want to know that Carson Culbert is dead."

# Twenty

"That was fast," I said to Noah once the call was over. "I told Jerica about the mug and Carson is dead in less than twenty-four hours. Remind me not to get Jerica mad at me."

Noah was skeptical. "You don't really think Jerica killed him."

"You watch the same cop shows I do," I said. "If the deceased is married, the surviving spouse is always the primary suspect."

"Or she's sleeping with the suspect," Amara said. "Cop shows use that one a lot. It's a regular trope in the cop show genre. I remember this one episode of..."

"Focus, Amara. Focus," I reminded my easily distracted friend. "Officer Singer said Theresa called an ambulance right after she found Carson. The medical examiner must have been riding along with the paramedics because he was the one who called the police, not the family. Carson was dead when the ambulance arrived, if he wasn't already."

"And Valena's doctor boyfriend?" Noah asked.

"The ambulance beat him there," I said. "Singer said Dr. Hickner showed up just as they were zipping up the body bag." I wondered if the doctor made his usual house call the night before but left before the ambulance arrived that morning. I didn't think he was living there, but he might as well have been.

I could see the outline of Amara's tongue as it pushed hard against her cheek. "Valena must not have gotten to her phone fast enough. Did the police say whether there would be an autopsy?" she asked.

"You mean unlike the first time?" I said. "Officer Singer said the medical examiner took the body straight to the morgue for an autopsy."

Officer Singer didn't say how or when this happened or where he as calling from. Given how Officer Singer and the rest of Boulder Police Department felt about me playing detective, I was surprised he called me at all. Maybe that was Singer's way of getting me to do the

hard work for him. Like last time.

I got what seemed like an urgent text from Destiny. *Need to talk. Not here. Where?*

I texted back. *At my cart on Pearl Street. In an hour?*

Several minutes passed before I got a reply. I was beginning to think that would be the extent of our conversation. My phone dinged again. It was Destiny.

*"One hour. I'll be there."*

"I've got to get dressed," I told my breakfast companions. "Destiny wants to talk."

I sat at my cart for about thirty minutes before Destiny showed up. I spent my time doing some sketches of lampposts, trashcans, anything I could find that did not remind me of drawing people. I suddenly understood the artistic appeal of painting landscapes and still life.

Destiny walked up, wearing her usual black attire but looking more disheveled than usual.

"You missed it last night," she told me. "Jerica and Carson had this big fight. I thought she was going to throw him down the stairs."

"Jerica would certainly be able to do that," I said.

"No kidding," Destiny said. "Hickner had to break it up."

"And did it get quiet after that?" I asked.

"It was until Theresa found Carson dead in the kitchen early this morning. Then the ambulance came, then the police. It was like Mother's death all over again."

"Do you think Jerica did it?" I asked.

Destiny thought for several seconds before she answered. "She could have. As angry as she was and as strong as she is, she could have easily snapped his neck. But there was no broken neck. There were no signs of a fight or anything like that. The only thing unusual, other than Carson laying there dead in the middle of the kitchen, was one of those orange syringes cap they found under one of the cabinets. The police took it as evidence."

Officer Singer had not shared that bit of information. I wondered what else he had not shared. I tried to think of why some-

one in the Menken house would have a syringe.

"Are any of you diabetic?"

"No," Destiny said. "And neither was Mother. The cap was all they found. No syringe. No medication bottles or anything that would give any clue about what was in there. But Officer Singer seemed sure that whatever was in the syringe was what killed Carson."

My phone rang as I was listening to Destiny. It was Theresa. I thought about what I should or should not say before I answered. "Does anyone know you're here?" I asked Destiny.

"No," she said.

"Then don't say anything," I told her. I put the phone on speaker so Destiny could hear.

"Good morning!" I said to Theresa while I looked at Destiny and pretended I didn't know Carson was dead. "Sorry I'm running late. I was about to come over." Destiny frantically waved her hands for me to stop talking. Or at least to not talk about going to their house.

Theresa cleared her throat. "I'm afraid we're going to have to put the portrait on hold for now," she said.

I kept pretending I didn't know about Carson's death. "Is everything okay?"

"Not really," she said. "I'll explain later. Today is just not a good day. I'll call you when I know what's going on."

I grabbed for any excuse that would get me back in the house. "If it's going to be a few days, then would you mind if I came over and grabbed my paint brushes and paints?"

Theresa's hand covered her phone. I could tell she was talking to someone, but I couldn't tell who. Probably Alyssa.

"I guess so," she said when she turned her attention back to the phone. "Just come in and get what you need and then go. We won't be painting any time soon." Theresa ended the call without mentioning Carson's death.

"What do you think?" I asked Destiny once she had put her phone down.

"You would have found out more if you had talked to Jerica," Destiny said. "Theresa didn't seem to want to talk."

"But she is the one who called," I reminded Destiny. "Alyssa hasn't called me. Valena didn't call."

I called Officer Singer back. Once again, I put the phone on speaker so Destiny could hear.

"I talked to Theresa Menken," I told Officer Singer. "Why do I get the feeling you left out some details about what happened to Carson?"

"Because I did," he said. "We're not going to share our investigation with you."

"Maybe I should adopt that same policy," I said.

The police officer sighed. "This is against my better judgement, but we owe you one for the Pello case. I'll tell you what we know. Then we'll be even. No more after that." He paused for a moment then spoke very softly. "The detectives tried to talk to all the Menken sisters but they called Alyssa and lawyered up. Suspects tend to do that rather quickly when they're looking at murder charges."

I looked at Destiny. "Did the detectives talk to everyone?"

"Every one except Destiny," Officer Singer said over the phone. "She apparently left before they got to her. If you see Destiny, you might want to let her know that the police want to talk with her. Her disappearing like that only makes her look more suspicious. Not even her lawyer sister can help her with that."

Destiny closed her eyes and shook her head.

"If I see her, I'll do that," I said. "You still haven't told me what you know. Did your medical examiner find anything in Carson's blood?" I asked.

"Should he have?" Officer Singer replied. "Talk to me, Gabriella. What do you know?"

"I don't know anything," I lied. "I assumed that a forensic toxicology report would be standard procedure in a case like this. Was I wrong?"

"No, you were right," he said. "It's part of the autopsy." Officer Singer paused, as if he was considering the height of the ledge
he was on before he jumped into the abyss.

"The blood work came back about an hour ago," he said. "The victim had ethylene glycol and ketamine in his system when he died. There was a needle mark on his neck."

I was intimately familiar with ethylene glycol. "Tell me about ketamine," I said.

"I don't know what doctors use it for," Officer Singer admitted, "but our people use it as a chemical restraint for people who pose a danger to themselves or others. Or if we just don't want to deal with them and need to shut them down for a while. You may know it as 'Vitamin K', a date rape drug."

"Where would you get something like that?"

"You can buy it online," he said. "Not legally, of course. They're only supposed to sell it to licensed healthcare providers, usually hospitals and clinics. But you know how it is. If you want something bad enough, you can find it. You can also get a prescription for it, but that's not very common."

"You said only one needle mark. Did the killer inject the ethylene glycol?" I asked.

"No," he said. "That would require at least a three ounce syringe. Those are huge and it would take too long to inject. The victim would fight back before you could make the injection. Our theory is that someone had been giving him EG for some time, basically doing to Carson what you claim they did to Mrs. Menken. It looks like someone got impatient. They got tired of waiting on the antifreeze, so they sped the process up with ketamine."

"This wasn't a spontaneous crime of passion," I said. "This was thought out."

"Ah, the infamous crime of passion," Singer said. I could literally picture this cop leaning back in his chair, swiveling back and forth while swinging the cord on the landline phone like a jump rope. "What is passion, Gabriella?"

"I'm sure I wouldn't know," I said.

Something about the tone of his voice made me throw up a little in my mouth. He laughed. "Not exactly passion," Officer Singer said. "This was more like the consummation of an affair after some heavy flirting. The ethylene glycol had been going on for a few days, small doses over maybe a week or more." He paused. "That ketamine injection probably was spontaneous, or as spontaneous as something like that can be. They had to get the needle ready and wait for Carson to be alone. That much was premeditated. But the exact moment probably was not planned. Someone saw an opportunity and took it. Or Carson crossed some line and made someone mad enough to finish it."

Destiny and I looked at one another again but said nothing.

"Thanks for letting me know," I said.

"Just don't tell anyone you heard it from me," he said. "And that makes us even. No more hot tips."

"I wouldn't expect any," I said. I ended the call and looked at Destiny.

"Who do you know that would have access to ketamine?"

# Twenty-one

Destiny and I were hoping that with everything going on we could sneak into the Menken house unnoticed. We were wrong.

Alyssa was talking to Valena and Theresa when Destiny and I walked in. Alyssa stopped mid-sentence. The lawyer-sister was not happy to see us. Valena simply got up and left the room.

"You should not have left before the police arrived," Alyssa told Destiny. "They want to talk to you and they're not going to like it if they have to track you down to do it. If you had stayed here, you could have avoided that." I wasn't sure if Alyssa would have defended Destiny even if she had been there. There seemed to be a very clear message that Destiny was on her own.

"And you." Alyssa's narrow eyes were looking square at me. "I thought I heard Theresa tell you that the painting was on hold." She was in full lawyer mode and exuded all the warmth and charm associated with the legal profession.

"She did," I said. I started to remind her that Theresa said I could retrieve my brushes but decided against it. "And I'm sorry. I left some things upstairs that I need. Would you mind if I went up there and got them? I won't be a minute."

Theresa looked at Destiny but was clearly speaking to me. "I suppose Destiny told you what happened last night. We are all very upset. It's frightening to know that someone broke into my home and killed a member of my family." She turned to me. "I just hope the killer doesn't come back."

I did my best to act surprised. "Did the police offer to put you in protective custody?"

Before Alyssa could answer, Valena appeared at the top of the stairs with a pistol in her hand.

"Valena!" Alyssa said. "What are you doing with Dad's gun?"

"This is my protective custody," Valena announced. She tried to twirl the pistol cowboy style but dropped as she came down the stairs.

"Valena, don't be ridiculous," Alyssa said. "No one is going into custody of any kind, protective or otherwise. Put Dad's gun away before you kill somebody."

"Unfortunate choice of words," Destiny said. No one laughed.

Alyssa ignored her sister and glared at me. "Get what you need and then go, Ms. Alegré."

Although it wasn't as I intended, my excuse for coming over wasn't simply an excuse to get inside the house. I was looking for something, anything, that would explain Carson's death. And I really did need to get my brushes and my paints, especially if the painting was on hold or eventually canceled altogether. I couldn't imagine that Valena or anyone else would want a four-foot by six-foot reminder of two family deaths and their killer hanging above the couch. Then again, I can't imagine hanging a taxidermied moose head with its glassy eyes staring at me from above my fireplace either. A trophy is a trophy, I guess.

"Thank you," I said. Destiny and I went upstairs. I heard Jerica softly crying behind her closed bedroom door as we walked down the upstairs hallway to the studio. I quietly knocked on the door to see how she was doing.

"Jerica?"

"Yes. Give me a second." Jerica opened the door, but did not invite me into the room. The grieving widow seemed happier to see me than her sisters had been.

"I heard what happened," I said. "I am so sorry."

"Thank you," Jerica said. She tried to smile through her tears. "I don't think I'll be sitting for a portrait today. Or maybe ever again. I'm going to go back home. There are things I need to do."

"Oh, no," I said. "I would not expect to paint anyone today." I brushed over the part about her leaving to go back to the ranch. "Do they know what happened?"

Jerica opened the door a little wider, but not much. "I don't know what they know," she said. "I'm sorry, but I really don't feel like talking right now." She wiped her eyes. "I'm going to take a walk. I just need to get away from here for a while."

"Of course," I said. "I'm sorry."

Jerica stepped out into the hallway and headed for the stairs. Destiny and I went to the studio to get my brushes and paints. I couldn't help looking at the half-done painting one last time. Neither could Destiny.

"For only one color, this is amazing," she said. "I would hang it up just like this."

"Thank you," I said. "But once I start something, I like to finish it." I sat down in the chair. "Did you find anything on your videos?"

"Not yet," said the resident videographer. "I've looked, but this is not a surveillance system. It's not like I have a camera in every room all the time. The security cameras are around the outside of the house but that's it. The only cameras I use are my big Canon that I use most of the time and my phone. I can really only record what's happening around me. Nothing else."

"You've never just set it up and let it run?" I asked.

"Never," was the flat reply. "Too risky. I've heard enough lectures from Theresa about invading their privacy already. Theresa would probably smash my camera if she found it."

"But surely you caught some conversations, someone talking or doing something," I said. I couldn't believe that the police had not already asked Destiny about her videos. Maybe they didn't know. Or maybe that was why Officer Singer wanted to talk to her.

"Could you send those videos to me?" I asked. "I could use some good original programming that doesn't require a subscription."

"I can get them right now," she said. She pointed to the large screen on the wall. "Maybe we can see more details if we watched them on that. I'll go get my computer."

I turned the chairs to face the screen and got ready to watch hours of Menken home movies, or at least until Theresa chased us out of the room. The only thing missing was popcorn. And the family. I looked at the screen that hopefully would provide some answers on Destiny's videos. It was either some bargain basement brand I'd never heard of, which was unlikely, given my familiarity with bargain basement brands, or it was some high-end, cutting-edge technology of

which I was not aware, a very strong possibility for someone who did most of her shopping at big box discount stores. Noah would probably know. I'd have to ask him later.

Valena was right. A person could live comfortably without ever leaving that room as long as they had some way to get food. I wondered how many meals Valena ate in here when she was in high school. I could picture Destiny sneaking food to her banished sister. Did it ever come to that?

The short walk to Destiny's room and back was taking longer than I expected. I peeked into hallway to see if she was coming but no one was in the hall. The door to Destiny's room was closed. If she was in there, she didn't want her sisters to know. I wondered if her computer was downstairs where she would have encountered Theresa or, even worse, Alyssa.

I made a note to ask Theresa about the canvas and what she wanted to do with it. I understood why she would not want it in her home – too many bad memories – but I hated to see that canvas and my work go to waste. Maybe I could keep the canvas if I promised to paint over it. It wouldn't fit in our place, but it would fit very nicely in Hempy's. I needed to talk to John Spool about when I could move in there. Talk about a lucky break.

More than the painting, I wanted to know who murdered Mrs. Menken. Carson had been my Suspect Number One, but he was out of the picture. It had to be the same killer for both. What are the odds of two murderers being in the same house, much less the same family? Dr. Hickner certainly seemed like a possibility. He had access to syringes and to ketamine. He certainly spent enough time in the house. But why would Hickner do it? Don't doctors take an oath to "do no harm" or something? Murder would seem to be a violation of that oath. Then again, an oath without a penalty didn't seem like much of a deterrent. People make promises they don't intend to keep all the time.

I intended to keep my promise to Alyssa to find her mother's killer, even if Alyssa hadn't been particularly friendly when I saw her this morning. Stress will do that to people, and all of these women had

been under stress for as long as I had known them, which, admittedly, was not that long but still, there was a lot of stress. Jerica's tears seemed very genuine when I saw her crying in her room. Not that murderers couldn't cry, but Jerica didn't seem like the type to kill someone. She certainly did not seem like the kind of person who would be satisfied with a slow death from ethylene glycol poisoning. If Jerica was going to kill, it would be a quick and sudden death. She'd probably just twist your neck and break it in one snap. And then go have a beer.

Theresa seemed more likely than Jerica. The house, the Will, her resentment about taking care of her mother, if she even had to do that. There seemed to be some question about whether Mrs. Menken was even in any kind of real decline when she was killed. Did Theresa lie about her mother's health to make her death seem more natural?

Then there was Valena. Her mother had cut off her financial support and probably cut her out of the will. She was seen more as a servant than a sister, with the whole "Valena, be a dear..." routine. Even beyond that, there was something cold about Valena. Destiny may have been debilitatingly shy around her family, but there was some genuine warmth there. Some compassion. I did not feel that with Valena.

And the doctor still didn't really make sense as a suspect, unless he did it for Valena. Men have been known to be persuaded to do stupid things, including murder. But it didn't feel right.

"You did it," I said to Valena's face in the painting. "But you're not going to get away with it." I found myself smiling, which seemed kind of wrong but there was a sense of accomplishment, a sense of satisfaction for figuring it out.

"Sorry to interrupt your conversation," Destiny said quietly. She ignored the fact that I was talking to a portrait. "I have the computer."

"Great," I said. I kept looking at the unfinished painting while Destiny set up the computer so we could go through no telling how many hours of video looking for some small detail that might be a clue.

Then I heard the door shut and the click of the lock.

I sprung towards the door and tried to open it, first by trying the doorknob and then with more drastic measures that only confirmed what I already knew. The door was locked. I put my feet on the wall and pulled on the doorknob as hard as I could. If I couldn't open it, then maybe I could pull off the doorknob and unlock it from there. But it was no use. Destiny's efforts to open the door were just as futile as my own. In one last act of desperation, I threw myself against what I soon learned was a solid door. Aside from a very sore shoulder, I got nowhere.

The door was not going to budge.

Like Valena and Jerica before me, Destiny and I were locked in.

# Twenty-two

"Jerica! Theresa!" I shouted. "Somebody! Help!"

I ran to the window and saw Theresa hugging Jerica in the driveway. I tried to open the window, but that portal was no more yielding than the door had been. I yelled but the women on the driveway below didn't seem to hear.

Destiny dropped into the chair. "Mother painted the windows shut," she reminded me. "They're not going to open. And that glass is unbreakable. Valena and I learned that when we were kids."

I pounded on the glass, but Theresa and Jerica were already too far away. I watched as they walked down the driveway and disappeared behind the trees, along with any hope of a quick rescue.

"They'll be back soon," Destiny said. She seemed rather nonchalant about being held captive. My guess was that this was not the first time she'd been locked in that room, either intentionally or, I was sure, by accident. "It will be only a few hours at the most," Destiny said. "We'll just have to wait."

I tried to think of a context in which "a few hours" qualified as "soon" but nothing came to mind. Maybe a few hours constituted a short time in the grand cosmic scheme of things. But there was a kind of theory of relativity at work. While a few hours felt like no time at all when I was with Noah or when I was painting, the prospect of spending even one more minute trapped in a room not of my choosing seemed interminable on our side of the locked door, even with all the sunlight and a well-decorated bathroom.

Destiny seemed to be resigned to our situation. "We might as well watch the videos and see if there's anything I missed. They'll be back eventually," Destiny said.

I got the feeling she'd been locked in this room before. Perhaps she wasn't sentenced to complete captivity like her two sisters, but the occasional teenage timeout certainly seemed like a possibility. Or maybe she had been locked in by one of her sisters as a joke. Or by accident. Either way, Destiny did not seem to share my concerns about our immediate futures.

I attributed her relative serenity to the fact that no one had tried to kill her recently. I, on the other hand, was trapped in the same room where someone tried to poison me only a few days before. It was not a pleasant memory nor an experience I cared to repeat. I looked at the windows and wished I had my mallet and screwdriver with me so I could chisel away and break the paint that sealed it shut.

Unless the door closed and accidentally and somehow locked itself, which did not seem likely, then whoever locked us in this room had to be the killer. Destiny was with me, so it couldn't have been her. Alyssa probably wouldn't do something this rash, although I knew from personal experience that lawyers are not immune from being crazy. But Alyssa didn't seem like the type of passively lock someone in a room. Jerica and Theresa were already out of sight when Hickner's car sped up the driveway.

Valena was the only sister unaccounted for. I remembered how she dropped her father's pistol as she tried to make her dramatic entrance on the stairs. Was Valena holding a gun on the other side of the door?

I watched out the window as Dr. Hickner pulled into the driveway and screamed Valena's name as he ran to the house. From just outside the studio door – the locked door – we heard Valena yell, "Up here."

Destiny's eyes shot to the door at the sound of her sister's voice. I watched as she reverted back to the withdrawn, silent creature that I met the night her mother died. The interesting conversationalist I had come to know was gone. In her disassociated state, Destiny was not going to be any help.

"I guess we know where Valena is," I said to Destiny. It wasn't exactly breaking news. Theresa and Jerica were gone. Destiny was with me. Alyssa was leaving when I came in. Valena was the only sister left in the house. Hers was the only voice we heard, other than Hickner.

I moved closer to the door so I could hear anything that she or her doctor boyfriend might say. I was not disappointed. Valena may have been our quiet captor, but the doctor was loud enough for both
of them. He did not sound happy.

"How many more, Valena?" he said. "How many more?"

"What makes you think there were any?" Valena asked her boyfriend. "Do you think I killed Mother and Carson? Maybe you should be in there with them."

"Of course, he thinks that," I screamed from my side of the door. "He's not an idiot. That's why he didn't order the autopsy for your mother. He didn't know for sure and he didn't want to take any chances in case it was you, right Doctor? He didn't order an autopsy because deep down, he knew you killed her. He just didn't want to admit it. Not to us and not to himself."

I waited for a reply but heard nothing from Valena or the doctor. I just hadn't hit the right nerve.

"And Carson?" I said to the door. "Doctor?" I used his title to remind him of the larger responsibilities that came with his oath as a doctor. "Did you help her kill Carson, too? Too bad you couldn't stop the autopsy on him. Your girlfriend got impatient and decided to go on without you. That happens when you get overconfident."

Again, silence from the other side of the door.

I leaned against door and hoped my voice was more effective than my shoulder had been at getting through the solid wooden barrier.

"And what about me, Doctor?" I said in as normal of a tone and volume as I could manage. "Too bad you weren't the doctor on call for the ER that night. Would you have put whiskey up my nose? Or would you have poured yourself a drink and finish what Valena started?"

Nothing. Silence.

What was it that Alyssa had told me? That Valena couldn't plan anything? It was very clear that she had no plan for what might happen once she locked us in the room.

I played the only card I thought I had left.

"Valena, did you know Destiny is in here with me?"

"Destiny?" Valena called out for her sister. "Is that true? Are you in there?"

Destiny's eyes delivered a soliloquy fit for a Greek tragedy. Unfortunately, her voice said nothing.

"She's not really talking right now," I said. "I'm kind of worried about her. She does not look good."

"You're lying," Valena said. "She's not in there."

I sat down beside Destiny. "I really need you to say something. Please." Destiny closed her eyes and took a deep breath.

Destiny squeezed my hand and somehow managed to speak. "I'm here, Valena."

I didn't know what Valena had in mind, but my objective was to keep her right where she was until Theresa or Jerica got home. I didn't like being locked in the room, but at least we were safe as long as Valena was on the other side of the door.

We didn't hear Valena's voice again for several minutes. I was beginning to think that telling her Destiny was in the room had bought me some time, if not a complete reprieve.

Then the door opened. In a black wig and wearing one of Destiny's dark outfits, Valena looked exactly like her sister, all the way down to the large silver cross hanging around her neck. She tossed a blonde wig with a peach streak to Destiny.

"Put this on," Valena told her. "Trust me, it will be an improvement."

We were also face to face with the late Mr. Menken's Ruger revolver. Valena pointed the gun at me and waved it towards the empty stool where each sister sat for their part of the portrait. Destiny gasped and pulled her knees to her chin.

"Have a seat," Valena said to me. "Right there."

I looked at the doctor, who seemed almost as confused as I was. "I take it you're not here to provide first aid?"

"I didn't think it would come to this," he said. "I thought there was a possibility with the others, but I didn't believe it."

"Do you believe it now?" I asked Hickner. "Because this seems very believable to me."

Valena smiled at the doctor. "Wow, you are gorgeous. Too bad you're so dumb. How did you even make it through med school?"

Valena's valid observation did not inspire confidence in my prospects or those of the American healthcare system. "Now, be a dear and stand over there by the artist."

I forced myself to laugh. "That's your big plan? To pretend to be your sister?" Destiny's eyes begged me to stop talking, even if her voice was out of commission. I ignored the request and kept saying whatever came to mind. I was trying to buy enough time for Theresa and Jerica to get back from their walk. "You really didn't think this through, did you?"

Destiny swallowed hard and put on the wig. Except for differences in their makeup, she looked just like Valena. Then she spoke.

"The Will," Destiny said softly. "You won't get anything anyway." Then she retreated back to wherever it was she went at times like this.

"You mean the Will that I forged to make it look like Theresa did it?" Valena said. The cruelty in her voice, even when speaking to her twin, was haunting. Her laugh was even more so. "You kind of messed up that part of my plan with all this, but I couldn't pass up the opportunity to lock you in here." No judge is going to accept that. Besides, it doesn't matter. As Destiny Menken, I'll withdraw all the money you've hoarded over the years plus whatever Mother left for you in the real Will, if she left you anything at all. I'll be the surviving twin in an unsolved series of tragic murders." Valena took a deep breath and smiled. "Talk about social media clout! I'll be the ultimate influencer."

Our captor looked at her sister. "Fix your wig. You look terrible. If you're going to be me, you have to step up your game. Even if you're dead." Destiny obediently did as she was told.

Valena moved the gun from human target to human target as she stepped backwards towards the door. "Who wants to be first?" she asked. The barrel was pointing at me when she stopped.

I heard a click.

Then another.

And another.

"It's not loaded," I said. I pounced on the small, would-be shooter and knocked her to the floor. The good doctor, to his credit, also lunged on top of her, pinning her body beneath his, something I suspect he'd done multiple times before but in a totally different context. Destiny came out of her catatonic state long enough to grab the gun when Valena dropped it. The darker twin pointed it at her sister.

"You never were much of a planner," the real Destiny said.

I put my hand on the gun barrel and lowered Destiny's arms. "I know that's not loaded," I said to Destiny. "But let's not get too carried away."

We were still trying to decide what to do with Valena when we heard Jerica and Theresa come through the front door. I ran to the stairs.

"Come here! Quick! We need you."

Jerica ran up the stairs with Theresa close behind. They stopped when they saw the scene in the studio.

"What happened here?" Theresa asked.

"Here's who killed your mother," I said. "By gradually putting ethylene glycol into her drinks, starting when Avyanna told her she was ending her allowance and timing it so the fatal final dose came when everyone was here so there would be more suspects." I turned to Valena. "You even asked for an autopsy to deflect suspicion from you. And I have to admit, I thought Carson did it, at first. But then you got greedy or something. Plus, I think you just didn't like the guy. I didn't like him either, but I didn't kill him. That's just cold."

I looked at Jerica. "Sorry. I just think you can do better. Much better."

Valena kept her eyes on me as she spoke to Jerica. "I will agree with Gabriella on that one." She quickly looked at Jerica. "You could do much better than Carson. But you weren't going to divorce him. We both know that he would have ended up with whatever money Mother left for you. I couldn't let that happen." She smiled. "But, if I'm being honest, killing Carson was more about stopping him from getting a part of my inheritance than it was getting rid of him for you."

I turned back to Valena. "So, you started working on killing Carson just like you killed Avyanna. And when he didn't drink the poison fast enough for you, you sped up the process with ketamine. But you're so used to people cleaning up after you that you didn't even think to pick up the syringe cap when you dropped it." I took a step closer. "What did he finally do that made you want to get it over with?"

Valena was still indignant. "I'm not saying anything until I've talked to my lawyer," she said. "Theresa, would you be a dear and call Alyssa?"

"Right after I call the police," Theresa said. "But I wouldn't count on much legal representation from Alyssa. She does contract law, remember? She doesn't do murder cases."

"I recommend Bruce Carlin," I suggested. "He was John Spool's lawyer on the Pello case. He's exactly the kind of attorney you deserve."

Valena must have realized she wasn't getting away from Hickner's grip because she stopped struggling to get free. I put my face next to hers.

"But what I can't figure out is whether you meant to kill me or if that antifreeze in my mug was meant for Jerica," I said. She rolled her eyes up at me. Her expression said it all.

"So, it *was* me," I said. "Thought so."

"We hired you to paint a portrait," she said. "Not to send one of us to prison, and especially not me."

I looked at Theresa. "Now we just have to figure out what to do with her until the police arrive."

Theresa's eyes narrowed in rage at her sister.

"We can leave her in here. Let me get my key."

# Twenty-three

"And that's how it happened," I said to Amara, Noah, and Paul as we had a celebratory dinner at Papa's Tapas. I had my personal favorite, the bacon-wrapped dates.

Amara raised her glass. "To happy endings," she said.

"I wouldn't really call it a happy ending," I told her. "How about just, 'to endings', happy or otherwise?" We clinked our glasses together.

"What's going to happen to the painting?" Noah wanted to know. "That was a lot of work."

"Oh. That." I put down my glass. "It was destroyed. We locked Valena in the room. By the time the police got there, she had thrown paint all over the canvas. Poor thing looks like some kind of Renaissance meets Jackson Pollock abstraction. Theresa said I could have the canvas. I just have to check with John about when I can move it into Hempy's."

"Speaking of John." Amara put her glass down. "I talked with him today while you were out fighting crime. Hempy's all moved out." She held up a worn brass key. "The bottom floor is ours for the taking."

"Can we put the big canvas in there?" I asked.

"The canvas and anything else you care to add." Amara put her hand on my arm and looked around the table. "We are about to open the first combination art studio, art gallery, and dance studio on Pearl Street. All we have to do is come up with a name."

"And the upstairs?" I asked.

"John said he'd be leaving before the end of the month," Amara told me. "We can move in then."

The thought of John leaving put a damper on our celebration. I was more grateful for the apartment than I could even say, but I wished John didn't have to go.

I looked at my friends sitting around the table and thought about how we would look posed together on a 72x42 inch canvas.

# Other books by Bob Seay

## Cozy Mystery

Drawn to Murder: A Gabriella Alegré Mystery

"Gabriella Alegré believes she has found her calling in Boulder, Colorado, drawing caricature portraits and Conte crayon paintings of tourists on Pearl Street. But her blissful artistic endeavor takes a hit when one of her fellow street artists, a flute player named Pello Panagiotopoulos, is murdered… If you're a fan of whodunnit murder mysteries, you will have an absolute blast reading Drawn to Murder." - Pikasho Deka

## Literary Fiction

Dad

"Bob Seay dedicates his novel Dad "to all families with aging parents," and I cannot imagine a more accurate portrayal or one more moving." – Jon Michael Miller, Readers' Favorite.

"Dad features a modern and witty tone that makes for a well-balanced read…. Unlike other fiction writers, Dad by Bob Seay doesn't shy away from discussing mental, emotional, and spiritual difficulties in great detail." - David Reyes, The Book Commentary

- Winner Colorado Authors' League 2022 Literary Fiction Award

- Winner: 2021 IAN Book of the Year Awards ("Literary/General Fiction" category)

The Band Room

Bob Seay pits tribalism, anger, and hate against diversity, acceptance, and compassion while reminding us that everyone is doing the best they can.

"The Band Room by Bob Seay is a unique story of social injustice, racial unfairness, and family dysfunction to which every reader will relate. Seay's story is an essential addition to any school or classroom library and should be added to every teenager's reading list." – Lisa McCombs, Readers' Favorite.

"An unusual and thoughtful high school novel that charts the political awakening of a young football player as he wrestles with social ostracism, a fascist coach, and an alcoholic mother in crisis. Especially welcome in this genre is the novel's attention to the thoughts and motivations of its adult characters, who are as fully fleshed as the youngsters. Issues of race, gender, and sexuality are handled sensitively but without compromise. Here, "Black Lives Matter" is not an empty slogan but a crucial aspect of everyday life requiring ongoing commitment and struggle." – Jacob Levich

- 2021 Readers' Favorite Gold Medal Winner in the Young Adult - Social Issues genre
- Finalist in Young Adult Fiction for the 2021 Maxy Awards!